PENGUIN M
SHE BROKE UP, I DIDN'T!

DURJOY DATTA was born in New Delhi, India, and completed a degree in engineering and business management before embarking on a writing career. His first book—*Of Course I Love You!*—was published when he was twenty-one years old and was an instant bestseller. His successive novels—*Now That You're Rich!; She Broke Up, I Didn't!; Oh Yes, I Am Single!; If It's Not Forever; Till the Last Breath; Someone Like You; Hold My Hand*—have also found prominence on various bestseller lists, making him one of the highest-selling authors in India.

Durjoy also has to his credit two television shows, *Sadda Haq* (Channel V) and Veera (Star Plus), both of which have done exceedingly well on Indian television.

Durjoy lives in New Delhi, loves dogs and is an active Crossfitter. For more updates, you can follow him on Facebook (www.facebook.com/durjoydatta1) or Twitter (@durjoydatta).

Also by Durjoy Datta

Hold My Hand

*

Till the Last Breath

*

Of Course I Love You
Till I Find Someone Better

(With Maanvi Ahuja)

*

Oh Yes, I'm Single!
And So Is My Girlfriend!

(With Neeti Rustagi)

*

Now That You're Rich
Let's Fall in Love!

(With Maanvi Ahuja)

*

Someone Like You

(With Nikita Singh)

*

You Were My Crush
Till You Said You Love Me!

(With Orvana Ghai)

*

If It's Not Forever
It's Not Love

(With Nikita Singh)

She Broke Up
I Didn't!

I Just Kissed Someone Else!

DURJOY DATTA

Penguin
metro reads

METRO READS

USA | Canada | UK | Ireland | Australia
New Zealand | India | South Africa | China

Metro Reads is part of the Penguin Random House group of companies
whose addresses can be found at global.penguinrandomhouse.com

Published by Penguin Random House India Pvt. Ltd
7th Floor, Infinity Tower C, DLF Cyber City,
Gurgaon 122 002, Haryana, India

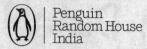

First published by Srishti Publishers and Distributors 2010
Published in Penguin Metro Reads by Penguin Books India 2013

ISBN 9780143421597

Typeset in Adobe Caslon Pro by Eleven Arts, Delhi
Printed at Thomson Press India Ltd, New Delhi

www.penguin.co.in

To the girl who had vodka bottles stashed
under her bed

Acknowledgements

Many people whom I thank below have unwaveringly stood beside me while I finished this manuscript in record time, guiding me, criticizing me and supporting me. I hope their efforts pay off. I thank Maanvi Ahuja, for always being there, no matter how stupidly or senselessly I have acted.

Sachin Garg for letting me know every day that I can kick some serious ass this time, Ekta Mehta for being so unrealistically sweet, supportive . . . and beyond awesome! Vaaruni Dhawan for being such an incredibly cute influence in my life, Neeti Rustagi for being with me all these years, Savvy Singh for the helping hand she has always extended, Rohini Khanna for fooling me into believing that I am worth something, Surabhi Guha Mazumdar for being the awesome person she is, Uttara Rao for being such a boost to my ego, Hansita for being the one who bears the brunt of my typos the most, Chhavi Kharuna for all the spiritual gyaan, Ankita Mehta for just being there!

I also thank these people for making my life as good as it is right now—Nikita Singh, Naman Kapur, Abhishek Sachdev, Nitin Verma, Aeshna Nigam, Vandana Vidyarthi, Anupriya Aggarwal, Ekta Bharadwaj, Farah Maheshwari, Farah Saxena, Varun, Neha Kakkar, Soumi Das, Shreyasi Bose, Medha Shree,

Nidhi Sharma, Gunjan Sayal, Rumpa Roy Chauhan, Neha Kakkar, Gunjan Upreti.

Arpit Khandelwal, Ankit Mittal, Abhishek Chopra, Ashish Rander, Eeshaan Sharma, Tigmanshu Dubey, Mukul Gupta for making college life at MDI what it should be like—awesome! I thank the entire batches of MDI PG '08 and '09, especially PG '09 Section C, simply because I love these guys.

Now to thank people who really matter—my extended family for they have always been there. And Guruji, because without his blessings all this would still have been a distant dream!

Prologue

The days were long. Long as they had never been. The air was still in the room. Nothing moved. It had been three days since I had locked myself in. It had been three days since I had broken up with Avantika. I read a page from my old diary, from three years back, where I used to recount every important day of my life, and the first time I had met Avantika was one of them.

There were other people in that incident, who were no longer in my life, but Avantika was and she always will be.

I guess . . .

September 2007

Today was a day when I spent most of my time with my eyes and mouth wide open. Avantika had just landed and my best friend wanted me to meet her.

I was told that Avantika had been in rehab for her drugs and alcohol problem but that was more than a year back. I had already started imagining Avantika as a leather-jacketed gothic chick with metal piercings and black nail paint.

And then, there she was . . .

That could have been the last thing I remembered from today had I had a weak heart. I had passed out for a few seconds for sure. My heart skipped a beat or maybe it just stopped beating altogether. I was choking. My stomach churned. I felt the blood rush down to the ends of my arteries and then burst out. I could feel my brain imploding. I was going to die and I was sure.

She is breathtakingly beautiful! She is a dream. Even better, you could not even dream of something so perfect. *Plastic surgeons still cannot rival God*, I thought.

She is so hard to describe. Those limpid, constantly wet black eyes and melancholic face screamed for love. The moonlight that reflected off her perfectly sculpted cheekbones seemed the only light illuminating the surroundings. Somebody stood with a blower nearby to get her long, black hair to cover her face so that she could look sexier flicking it away from her eyes. She has the big eyes of a month-old child—big and screaming for attention—a perfectly drafted nose, flawless bright pink lips and a smooth, pale complexion that would put Photoshop to shame.

Oh hell, she is way out of my league.

She was a goddamn goddess or she was the devil. She could not possibly be human.

I just could not look beyond her face.

I was not seeing right, I was not hearing right. I was just lost in the reflecting pools in those beautiful eyes. My heart pounded so hard it felt like it would pop out of my chest any moment. She asked me how I was doing; her voice was music to my ears.

Drugs? Alcohol? Leather? She would not even

know all that. I did see the remnants of a piercing just above her left eyebrow, and sure enough, a tattoo peeked out from under her sleeve: a red swastik sign. I told myself it was just a dream and I didn't just see the prettiest girl ever.

I managed to answer her in what seemed like my fourth attempt at speaking after the first three ended in some soundless flapping of my tongue. It was a strange feeling—I was nervous, shit nervous. I felt small. I felt ugly. I felt insignificant. I looked at her and smiled stupidly. I wondered if her dog looked cuter than I did.

I spent the evening trying not to stare into those fall-in-love-with-me eyes.

I like your nose, can I touch it? I wanted to say.

I like your lips, are they for real? I wanted to say.

I like your eyes, can I stare into them forever? I wanted to say.

I truly have not seen someone who is so perfect in her existence that you feel worthless and depressed. The simplicity of what she came wearing, the honesty in her smile, the serenading voice, the depth of her eyes—unforgettable.

It has been four hours since I took her leave but I cannot get her out of my head. That smile, those eyes . . . they are just not leaving me. As I sleep today, I wish to see her again. Soon.

This was the day that marked the end of my reckless dating days, when the only consideration while choosing a girl used to be whether she would kiss me or not. That day was different. I needed her.

It had been three and a half years since then, and I had fallen in love with Avantika every single day of the twelve hundred and seventy-five days that we had been together. I have been more in love with her every new day. Between that day and today, she has only got more beautiful, more charming, more adorable and lovelier.

Why me, of all the guys she could have dated? I had never managed to figure that one out. I closed my eyes and thought about what had got me here, alone and suicidal.

1

I had been tense for the last few days. Interviews for summer internships at Management Development Institute, Gurgaon, had started; Avantika and I did not want to go to different cities for our internships.

I had first met Avantika when I was studying engineering at Delhi College of Engineering and she was studying at Shri Ram College of Commerce. We graduated from our colleges, and joined the same firm in Hyderabad; things were going perfect for us. We were just twenty-two but had started planning our future together. On days when we were sure that we would always be together, she even told me what names she had decided for her kids. We were that serious.

It had been a while that we had been working when recession hit our firm and I was thrown out of the company. I worked for a smaller firm for a couple of months but it wasn't really the same. That is when we decided we needed to study further and started studying for the management entrance examinations. Three months later, we were at MDI, a top-rung management institution in Gurgaon, and we couldn't be happier.

I hadn't stayed away from her for a really long time now, and the prospect of going to different cities for our internship scared me.

'I am sure I will screw this one up,' I said, rubbing my sweaty palms together. The company had shortlisted fifteen students for the interview stage. They had planned to take just four. Avantika and I were among the last few in the preference order that the company had stated.

'You will not screw it up. Relax,' she said and rubbed my hands.

'But what if they take the first four guys and leave the campus? We might not even get a chance for an interview!' I grumbled.

Many companies did that. They did not want to interview a whole lot of people to choose their interns. They specified an order in which the students should come. If they liked the person, they would take him or her and close the placement process. The students lower down in the interview schedule often didn't get a chance!

'Let's hope for the best!' she said.

'Avantika? Rubbing your hand like that on my shoulder would only distract me,' I pointed out.

'You clear the interview and I will do it without your clothes on,' she winked.

'I won't get through.'

'You will. Trust me,' she said.

When two beautiful eyes look at you and say something with conviction, you cannot help but believe it. She smiled at me and it calmed my nerves a little.

The first interview was over. The guy came out smiling and with an offer letter in hand. My hopes died. There were just three more seats to fill up and there were ten interviews before me. There was no way Avantika and I were clearing this interview together.

'Now what!' I said.

'Relax, Deb. There are still three seats left.'

'And ten guys to interview! What if they choose even two?'

For the first time that morning, I saw her a little tense. 'I should go talk to the guy handling this thing.'

'What can he change?' I asked irritably.

'Let's see,' she said and handed over her file to me.

Avantika looked stunning that day. She seemed to have jumped out of a women's formal-wear fashion magazine: the short business skirt she wore looked fabulous on her, and a perfectly fitting blazer and shiny black pointed stilettos completed the power-woman picture. She made the clothes look good and not vice versa. There were whispers in the corridors of our college that morning, 'Obviously, she will get through! She is so hot!'

Avantika got up and walked up to the college representative who was handling the interview process. There were hushed whispers around me. I saw Avantika tell him something, her eyes stern, but her smile was in place.

'What is she doing?' I heard the guy sitting next to me ask his friend. Avantika talked to that senior for a little while, came back, and sat next to me.

'What was going on there?' I asked.

'Nothing. Just be prepared. You will be the next one to be interviewed. Do well,' she pulled up my tie.

What!

The guy from the interview room came out. He was not selected.

'Debashish Roy, you're next,' the college representative said.

I got up and entered the room. The whispers of other shortlisted students grew louder; no one was happy that Avantika had charmed her way into getting her boyfriend into the interview room.

No one said anything to her.

Avantika had always been intimidating for people who did not know her. One stern statement from her and the authority crushes you. One smile of hers and you are charmed, lost in those beautiful sparkling eyes and the dazzling smile. It had been three years and I was still trying to cope with these.

The interview was slightly long, but I had been taught well by Avantika. Soon, they slipped the offer letter in front of me. I signed the document and came out smiling. People looked at me, disgusted. 'Fuck you,' I muttered under my breath.

I sat there with Avantika and hoped no one else made it. The next few went in for the interview and no one got selected. *Eat that, motherfuckers*, I said in my head every time someone left that room without an offer.

Finally, they called Avantika in. There were still two seats left. And as expected, she came out flashing an offer letter.

'To my room,' she said, even before I could congratulate her.

Twenty minutes later, we were in her hostel room, wrapped around each other. Our well-ironed suits lay crumpled and strewn across the floor. Our bodies were a tangled heap, intertwined, our fingers wrapped around each other's. She was still wearing her stilettos. My socks had still not left my feet.

'That was good,' she said.

'Good? That was awesome.'

'Yeah. You were good. I was the awesome part of this entire session,' she winked.

I was still tired and panting from the lovemaking, when I saw a few tears in her eyes.

'Aw! What happened, baby?' I asked her.

'I heard someone call me a slut today,' she answered.

I knew people would talk. 'You're mine, baby,' I said.

'They don't matter anyway. We do,' she said and wiped off her tears.

'Just curious—what did you say to him?'

'I just requested him that since you have no other shortlists, you should be allowed in first. That this was your last chance at a decent internship . . .'

'Didn't he know that I had three more shortlists?'

'He forgot,' she smiled naughtily.

We kissed.

I was happy that we had got into the same company and were going to the same city for our internship, but I did not like that she had to flirt with someone to get it done. People talked about it for a few days and then forgot. It hurt her when people said things about her behind her back, but she tried not to show it.

Assholes.

2

'Hey!' I waved my hand from the lift lobby.

She looked, ignored my frantic hand movements across the hallway and went back to the computer screen. I walked slowly through the cubicles on both sides, and smiled at people who knew me and they smiled back at me. Most of them knew where I was heading to.

'Good morning,' I said. Her perfume wafted into my nostrils. The perfume was my third anniversary gift, three bottles of it, and she had vowed to wear it every single day. She had made the fragrance her own. Three days in a swampy tent in Ooty and she would still smell the same.

'What the hell were you doing there?' she asked angrily, not sharing my enthusiasm. Her frown and her wide open eyes didn't scare me; it just made her look more adorable. It's as cute as a puppy wrestling a rubber ball.

'I was just excited to see you.'

She turned away from me and flicked her hair behind her ear, 'You don't have to show the entire floor that you were excited.'

'What? Everyone knows that we are together,' I argued.

She had got fairer, if that was possible. Her nose looked a little red from the chill in the air; her lips a little more red and cheeks a little more pull-*able*. She looked gorgeous.

6

'Not the bosses. They don't know about us and they don't have to.'

'So what? What if they know?' I asked, as I pulled up a chair from the nearby desk.

'They are old people, Deb, they don't understand all this. Office romances are not seen in a kind light, Deb.'

'First of all, we are just interns here. And second, this is not a romance,' I said. 'This is just a fling. All I bear for you is unprecedented lust.'

She caught me in a gaze, her lips slightly parted, infinitely sexy. 'Is it so?'

'It sure is,' I said.

'Then you really don't mind,' she turned away from me and tapped on the keyboard, 'if I check out other guys' profiles on Facebook . . . Oh, I think this one is hot. Should I send him a friend request? He would be hot in bed too, I guess. But why look outside, when I have Kabir right here in the office?'

My heart shrank. Even as a joke, it wasn't funny. It didn't help that Kabir was taller, fairer, handsomer and more accomplished; also he had always harboured a soft corner for Avantika.

'Why, why, why would I mind? Go ahead. Sleep with him for all I care. I don't mind. Did I tell you about last night? Last night was awesome. Malini is incredible in bed. I mean, she is really good.'

Avantika looked at me, her eyes quivering and still big, 'Never say that.'

'You started it.'

'Never.'

'Okay.'

3

Avantika and I had been going out for quite a few years now, and except for one break-up that lasted a little while, it had been a smooth ride. Well, not really. The days were smooth, the nights . . . rough. I wasn't complaining. Three years and empty classrooms, hostel rooms, secluded roads and movie hall: things like these still excited us. We still couldn't keep our hands off each other, and we still acted like teenagers on a hormone overload. A girl like her had no business to even kiss a guy like me, but she did, and I was thankful for that.

'So, season eight?' she asked, fiddling through the rack of CDs.

'Whichever would do.'

'*The Man with the Long Stick*?' she asked.

'No, that is a little boring.'

'*The Turkey*?'

'No, that we have seen a million times.'

'*The Gas Burst*?'

'Umm . . . no.' I shook my head. 'Why don't we watch the fifth season, the third or the fourth episode?'

'Why didn't you say it in the first place?' she said, a little miffed.

'I like it when you ask.'

8

'Drama queen.'

She hit the play button. It was probably the hundredth time we were watching this episode, but I didn't mind. Every time, it was funnier than the last time. I had tried watching those sitcoms alone, but they were never as much fun as they were with her. She snuggled up to me, passed on the popcorn and closed her eyes. 'What do you think will happen tomorrow?' she asked.

'You will get the job, that's what,' I said.

'Are you sure?'

'Yes. There's absolutely no competition. You have worked nights on an internship. No one does that. You will be their first choice, Avantika.'

She felt a bit relaxed and hugged me tighter.

The next day was pretty exciting for interns like her who were expecting a pre-placement offer. Which meant a few interns will go back with an assured job in hand with still a year to go for college to end.

Avantika fancied her chances.

~

I couldn't wait to go back to college. It had been two months that I had been going to that monstrous building made out of steel and glass, wearing a suffocating tie, and I couldn't take it any more. Avantika, on the other hand, had been hyperventilating since the morning. We didn't exchange a single word till the time we reached office for the last day of our internship.

'It will be okay,' I assured her.

It wasn't until afternoon that the managers called all of us and gave us an extensive review on how each one of us had done during the internship. The reviews for Avantika and Kabir

stood out and their managers couldn't stop gloating over their
dedication and the hard work they had put in. I slept through
most of it. I just wanted to hear whether they would offer
Avantika a job or not. That's all I cared for. The conference
ended and we all walked out. We had expected that they would
announce the names of the interns they had chosen for a job
but they didn't. They said they needed more time to decide
since everyone was so brilliant. Obviously, they weren't talking
about me because my manager described my performance as
'he didn't miss deadlines'. He was a prick anyway.

'What do you think of the chances?' she asked.

'You will get through. Did you not hear what he said?
You were brilliant, and I didn't hear him say these words for
anyone else.'

'You are just being sweet,' she said. 'Even Kabir's manager
was so gung-ho about him.'

'Why would I be sweet?'

'Because that's what you are,' she answered. 'I'm so nervous.
I think I will pass out.' She kept chewing on her painted
nails. 'Deb, do you think we can go to the human resources
department and ask for the cheques of our stipends?'

'Is that what you want to do on your last day in this office?'
I asked.

'What do you have in mind?' Avantika asked. *Silly question*,
I thought.

A little later, we were walking to the conference room,
nervous and sweating. The people in the cubicles who looked
at us as we walked past them had no idea what was on our
minds. The walk of shame lasted an hour and my heart was
thumping. We bolted the door behind us.

'What if we get caught? This is not good,' she said.

'I know,' I answered and she put her hands across me. 'But
this is my revenge for whatever the internship put me through.'

'They paid you while you sat at my desk doing nothing.'

'Oh, shut up,' I grumbled. 'Don't kill my anger. I'm really angry and I become a really good kisser when I'm angry.'

'Why haven't I ever felt that?' She chuckled.

I pulled her close. 'Whatever.'

The projector of the room was still running. Avantika killed the lights and darkness engulfed us. We were bat-shit scared, but the thrill of making out in an office conference room couldn't have been ignored.

Half an hour later, as we lay on the floor of the conference room, exhausted, she said, 'Let's go away, Deb.'

'Go away? Where?'

'Anywhere? Somewhere far from here. There are still five days to go for college and we have nothing to do.'

'We can just stay at my place and do nothing.'

'That's boring,' she said. 'Let's go to Goa? It's not that far! I have been so tense with the internship and the pre-placement offer. I deserve a break, don't I?'

'Are you serious?' I asked her because in the past two months I had suggested the same about three thousand times.

She rested her head on my shoulder. 'I'm serious.'

'Goa it is then! I just have a lot of packing to do,' I mumbled.

We smiled. Soon, we realized that we couldn't lay around naked in the conference room much longer. We got up, checked each other's necks for love bites, kissed each other one more time and headed back to our seats. A victorious smile broke out on my face.

4

I was really excited about the Goa plan, but packing weighed it down and I was more hassled than excited. Packing is not a very cool or a masculine thing to do. I got irritated in a while and called her up for help. My clothes were strewn all over the bed, the dining table, the washroom . . . they were everywhere, and I didn't know where to start. Avantika had already packed and was on her way to my place. I panicked, grabbed hold of all the clothes and stuffed them inside two suitcases, and there were still boxers, socks and trousers, waiting to be folded and packed. Somehow my clothes had expanded during the two-month stay and wouldn't fit in the two suitcases they had come in. I gave up. It was a lost cause.

'How much more time will you need to pack, Deb?' she asked as the cab driver piled up five of her seven suitcases neatly over one another in the drawing room.

'Avantika? Exactly how many clothes do you have?'

'Leave that,' she snapped and paid the cab driver.

She was positively shocked when she entered my flat; she looked around like she had stepped in a post-war Nazi camp with bodies lying around, decomposing. It was a rotting bachelor's pad, and I had done well to keep her away from it during our internship.

'This smells like a rotting crime scene,' she grumbled.

'Why do you think I spend more time at your flat than mine?' I asked. She was rolling up her sleeves. 'You don't have to bother with that, Avantika. Let's just pack and leave.'

It was already too late; she was already mopping. She was an obsessive cleanliness freak. A speck of dust and she would rush to dust the whole room, one soiled pair of boxers in one corner of the room, and she would make it her agenda to get my whole wardrobe washed. The only reason why my room in the MDI hostel was probably the cleanest of all rooms, including the girls' rooms and excluding hers, was Avantika.

'Deb, is this how you pack?' She yanked open the suitcases and the clothes spilled over. It was like the suitcase threw up all over her. 'And you have mixed all your stuff. These are so smelly. And don't just sit around there. Come and help me with this.'

I walked up and pretended to fold clothes and jammed them into suitcases.

'You are doing nothing, Deb. Just go and do whatever you want to do,' she said angrily. Not wanting to piss her off more, I just sat there and looked at her as she neatly segregated the clothes and then placed them in different bags and suitcases, her face constantly crumpled due to the ungodly smell.

'It's insane that you can look so great even while you're packing clothes into a suitcase,' I remarked.

'Shut up and don't distract me,' she said. I could sense her smiling even as she pretended to be angry.

'I am done,' she said.

The bags and suitcases were done, the wardrobes were empty, the toiletries and the shoes had been packed, the utensils had been washed and the flat now looked habitable; it also stank less somehow.

'So, we leave now?' I asked.

'In a while,' she said. 'Let me catch some breath first.' She flopped down beside me. 'You're by far the dirtiest boy I have ever seen.' She breathed heavily.

I leaned in to kiss her but she slapped me away. 'Your mouth stinks of dead rat. Did you even brush today?' She scowled.

'I did!'

'You still smell like shit.' She laughed.

'Why don't you simply say you don't want to kiss me?'

'Didn't I do that just this morning?'

She pulled me by the collar and planted a long one on my lips. And as it happened every time, bolts of electricity ran through my spine as she pulled me deeper inside her mouth. Her sweet lips and rampaging tongue turned my world upside down every time they touched mine. She let me go while she still stared into my eyes.

'You taste terrible.'

'But you seem to like it.'

'I love it.'

~

The plan to Goa was cancelled, like every other plan. There was never a better plan than just being in her arms. She told me that she was tired and I told her that we should just hug each other, sleep and not leave the bed for the next five days. Avantika nodded like a little child and buried her head into my chest.

'So we are not going anywhere then, are we?' she asked, her eyes twinkling.

'Does it look like we are going?'

'Are we just sleeping?' she asked.

'Yes,' I said and made her lie down on a pillow.

'Where are you going? I need someone to hug,' she said adorably and my heart melted in unrecognizable blobs.

'I will just come.'

'Okay,' she said, rubbed her face on the pillow, closed her eyes and smiled.

I took a mental note—*burn the pillow, she loves it.* I returned with a ring I had bought for her with the stipend of our first months' internship. My friends advised me against getting her a ring because of the obvious symbolic connotations of buying a girl a ring, but I couldn't care less. If anything, I bought the ring for its symbolic connotations.

'Come here. I missed you already,' she said and pulled me inside the quilt, 'and go nowhere.' She kissed me.

'I am not going anywhere.' I kissed her back. 'I have something for you.'

'I want it if it is a long hug.'

'That too,' I said and fished it out of my pocket. 'This is for you.'

'What is?' she paused and took the little red box in her hand. She gingerly opened the box as if she would break it. 'Oh! This is beautiful, this is so beautiful!' she exclaimed, running her fingers over the tiny stone studded in a gold ring. 'Thank you so much, baby! Won't you help me wear it?' she asked.

Nervously, I slipped it on her ring finger, not worrying about what she would think I meant.

'I didn't know you had any taste in junk jewellery,' she nudged me.

Junk jewellery? Maybe I should have listened to my friends and not trusted my terrible taste in jewellery. I kept shut.

'Deb?' she said as I stared blankly at the ring, which had seemed beautiful to me when I bought it, but now looked awful. Why? It looked all right before. Even the over-eager salesgirl had said I had brilliant taste and that my girl would be very happy. *Liar*, I thought. *Scumbag*, I thought.

'This is real,' I said. 'It's not junk.'

'Real, as in?' she asked, a little puzzled.

'This is real gold, and this is a real stone. I got it from a nice place,' I said, dejected. 'Even the salesgirl told me that I had made a great choice. Is it that bad?' It almost never happens, but I was, like, teary eyed.

'Don't tell me. This . . .' she looked surprised. 'It is really nice.'

'You don't have to lie now. You just said it. Never mind, it is for you. You can get it changed if you want to,' I said, trying not to sound low. I added, 'I have the receipt, and if you see the salesgirl, smack her for me. That lowlife.'

'Deb? Are you crying?' she asked. 'Are you?'

'Me? No! No, not at all. Why? Why would I cry?' I asked.

'Aw! That's adorable.' She looked at me like I was a puppy run over by a minivan. 'I could tell you the item code of this ring, Deb. I know it's real. I was just joking! And I, absolutely, LOVE it!'

'I positively hate you,' I grumbled. The useless tear streaked down my cheek, washing away my masculinity.

'No, you don't hate me,' she responded. 'You wouldn't have given me this ring. Deb, this is very expensive.'

'Money's never an issue,' I said, my head held high in mock arrogance.

'I would just hate to marry a guy with no bank balance!'

'Marry?' I asked her. 'How many times do I have to say it is just lust?'

She snuggled up to me and whispered, 'For all the macho shit you pull on me, Deb, you're like a little child inside. You're like a soft toy with extra testosterone.'

'That has to go down in history as the strangest compliment, ever,' I answered.

'I know,' she said, closed her eyes and rested her head on my arm. 'You smell nice.'

She wrapped her arms around me and purred.

5

It was late evening when we woke up amidst the packed suitcases and nowhere to go. I was hungry, but too lethargic to reach out to the phone and call for food. Avantika's eyes were still closed, her lips quivering, half-awake, half-asleep. 'What do you want to do for the next three days, baby?' I asked her.

'Don't disturb me, let me finish the dream,' she said and turned away from me.

'It's not a dream if you are awake,' I said and she punched me. I waited for five minutes; her closed eyes fluttered and her lips curved into a small smile.

'What was the dream all about?'

'Nothing much, the usual,' she said.

'Either you don't tell me such things or if you do, complete them! Tell me what the dream was about?'

'Umm...we were...you know...kind of getting married,' she murmured. I was pleasantly shocked and infinitely happy that she, too, thought about the idea.

'So where was the wedding?' I asked.

'I don't know.'

'Who all were there?'

'I don't know,' she said. 'All I know is that it was a wonderful feeling. You were there. There was me, and a lot of flowers.

There were promises and the vows that we would always be together. Your parents were there too.'

'And yours?'

She didn't answer. It had been a year since she last talked to her parents—conservative idiots—and they had called her a disgrace since she was overage, unmarried and was dating somebody. For them, she was a commodity to be married off in a family that would accentuate their name, and more importantly, their business. She hadn't seen much of them since she started working.

'I'm sorry,' I said, finding nothing to add to her wedding dream. 'Hey, do you still want to go to Goa?'

'Nah, I just realized after two months of office that all I want is to stretch and relax,' she said.

'Umm . . . Aparna Di called when you were asleep. We can go to her place,' I said, wanting to cheer her up. 'It will be a change.'

Aparna was my crazy elder sister who got married a couple of years ago, and she knew about Avantika and me. There were more than a few reasons for me to believe she was fonder of Avantika. They had met just a couple of times but there was an undeniable mutual liking between them.

'She called me, too, in the morning. But I didn't give it a thought because we were going to Goa. Yes, we can. That would be nice.'

'You want to go?' I asked her.

'I would love to go. It's been like ages since I met her. And she has been asking for so long to meet up,' she said.

'That is probably because Arnab is out on a tour and she has nothing better to do.'

'Shut up! She just likes me so much,' she said. 'And you are just jealous that she likes me better.'

'Oh, please! Keep me out of such TV-soap-opera-type feelings!'

She laughed. 'So when do we leave?' she asked.

'Let us leave tomorrow.'

'Check the bus timings?'

'As you say,' I said, like a puppy would. 'The last thing I would do is try to argue with someone as pretty as you.'

'Men are not meant to win arguments,' she said.

'Yes, they are not.'

~

'I am so excited to see her,' she said, clutching my hand.

We took the next available bus to Pune, which wasn't until the next day. Aparna Di had been living in Pune since she got married and I had not seen her in the longest time. She had settled into the role of a wife more comfortably than I had imagined; she had been a problem child for all her life, spoilt and loved and boisterous and outgoing.

'Why? I have spent eighteen years with her and let me tell you, she is boring.'

'Did I ask you anything?' she said.

'By the way, Kabir called when you were loading your baggage. He wanted to know our plans for the day. I told him we are going to Pune,' I said.

'Why didn't you give me the phone?'

'You were busy.'

'Oho!' she said and started tapping her phone. I was miffed at her eagerness to call Kabir back, the self-satisfied bastard. Luckily enough, the call didn't connect.

'You seem to be pissed,' she said and smiled.

'You know why. I don't like the guy. He's just . . . I don't want to talk about it.'

'No, let's talk about it.'

'I don't want to. It is better that we don't talk about a

guy who is probably better than me in every sense and likes my girlfriend.'

Being with Avantika was a constant battle; the feeling of insecurity never went away. I was just an average-looking guy with strange hair and a patch of beard on my chin. I didn't deserve a second look or a second date. Avantika always told me that she liked my dimple, but people usually missed it. No one, absolutely no one and that includes my mother, found me cute.

'He doesn't like me,' Avantika said.

'But he is better, right?'

'He is not better for me.'

'But he is better. If you were not with me, he would be your obvious choice. Or someone like him.'

Why couldn't she just lie that I was better! I never said Malini had better hair, or wore better shoes. It wasn't true, but still I wouldn't have said it even if it were true.

'Deb, if I were not with you it would not matter. But I am with you and for me, you are the best. I would prefer a shoe from a street-side shop than a Jimmy Choo that doesn't fit me.'

'Firstly, it's interesting to know that men are like shoes to you. And secondly, he's a Jimmy Choo and I'm a street-side shoe? What's next? That I'm a pair of slippers and he's a pair of stilettos?'

'You're taking the analogy too far,' she growled.

'You started it!'

'You are making me angry now,' she said, her eyes widening to show it.

'I'm sorry. I just don't like the guy. He's so good at everything he does, and he's fucking arrogant about it.'

She held my hand and calmed me down. 'By the way, how do you know he likes me?' she asked. 'Just curious.'

'I just know. It is evident. I have seen him look at you. He shuffles his feet and sweats and he's not his usual bastard self when he's with you,' I explained.

'But he has a girlfriend, Deb. And that is all he talks about.'

'So what? I can tell by the way he looks at you and drools. I don't blame him for that,' I said.

'Do you drool at other women too?'

'I am yet to come across a girl who is half as hot as you are. And I never move around without you. It is good for my ego to have you by my side. But yes, put Angelina Jolie with nothing on, that might stir something more than emotions,' I smirked.

'Good for you. I think there is an empty seat there. I will go there and from now on you can think of her and stir whatever you want to,' she said irritably.

'What? Why are you being angry?'

'I am not angry. I just want the best for you.' She smiled and tip-toed her fingers up my thigh. 'So who are you thinking about now? Angelina Jolie?' she smirked.

'Cancel Pune. Let's go back.'

6

The bus rolled into the city of Pune and we hired a taxi to my sister's place. Avantika slept through most of the bus journey and the taxi ride. When the taxi reached my sister's place, her hair was ruffled and her cheeks were puffed and she looked downright edible.

'I am kind of nervous,' Avantika said and combed her hair. 'Do I look fine?'

'It is not the first time you are meeting her. And you know she loves you a lot. I'm sure you two will get along.'

'You wouldn't understand.'

'Try me,' I said as I unloaded our bags, hers mostly.

'It is different now. I met her once, and that too when I was in college. It has been years. Things are different now'

'Twice, at the wedding too,' I added.

'That doesn't count.'

'It does. She liked your gift the best among hundred others. She said it was thoughtful and different. I was so happy that she said that. Even you were.'

'Deb . . . but she knows we are together now. Earlier, she just knew that we are friends.' I shrugged. 'And as usual, you are of no help at all.'

I rang the bell and heard footsteps moving towards the

door. It had been nearly a year since I had seen my sister. I had missed being around her, and I realized that when I heard the door click. My lips curved into a smile and then into a grin.

'Oh . . . look who is here! Finally got time?' she taunted.

'Yeah. And you have grown fat. The Bengali genes are finally kicking in,' I retorted.

'That doesn't work. I am still lighter than you.' She smiled back. 'Come in, Avantika. I like your scarf.'

She led us in, and after I stacked the suitcases in a corner, we sat down on the sofa. Aparna Di was a bit of a talker and for the good part of fifteen minutes she kept telling Avantika how beautiful she looked and how she always knew that I was smitten by her. The maid served us tea and biscuits and it was left untouched on the table as my sister went on and on about how she had reined in Arnab's bachelor instincts and had tamed him. I hoped Avantika was not noting down pointers.

'See, I don't really have to be formal with you guys. I'm a very bad wife and a worse host. So ask for anything, and the fridge is there, so help yourselves,' Aparna Di said and went into the kitchen to instruct the maid.

I noticed that she and Arnab were doing pretty well for themselves. The house was decked up with things from around the world and she looked happy and content. Since my sister was a bit of a crackpot, I hadn't given their marriage more than six months, so this was a welcome surprise.

'So, Avantika, how did you like Mumbai?' she asked.

'It was good, better than Delhi for sure. But I love this place too. It is so quiet.'

'I know. He always wanted a house away from the city.' Aparna Di smiled.

'How sweet!' Avantika said.

'So, if you guys were to pick a city to settle in, which one would you pick?' Aparna Di asked abruptly.

That question was strange enough to bring a smile to my face and a pink blush to Avantika's fair cheeks.

'C'mon, don't kid me. You guys have obviously thought about it,' she said. 'It's been a long time that you two have been dating.'

'Mumbai.'

'Delhi.'

She and I said respectively. We had talked about it a few times, but in our discussions it was either Singapore or Mauritius. Skyscraper-lit skies and the blue seas around us, a life of comfort, luxury and unending love.

'Discord already? Deb, Delhi? Avantika, Mumbai?' she smiled.

Avantika and I looked at each other and I turned. 'Mumbai is not that bad,' I said.

Aparna Di laughed.

'What?' I asked.

She kept laughing.

'What?'

'Avantika owns you. You're like a zombie slave to her,' she chuckled.

'I . . . am . . . It's not that,' I mumbled.

'Okay, whatever. That is your room. I am a little tired with all the cooking. I will go catch a nap. And, Avantika, I have a lot to talk about with you,' she said.

'Looking forward,' Avantika said and they hugged.

Aparna Di left us in the living room for her routine afternoon nap; it's a very Bengali thing to do—sleeping in the afternoons.

'I like your sister. She is fun,' she said as she dragged one of our suitcases to our room.

'I just find her boring and drab. It's been two decades. She is repetitive.'

'She is all parts of you, in a compact female form.' She smiled. 'I quite like her. I also really like this bed,' she said, with that drunken look in her eyes.

'I thought you said the kitchen slab.'

'I like that too.'

'I thought you like the bathtub.'

'I like that as well.'

'Why don't you say you like me?' I smirked.

'Maybe I don't. Maybe I just own you,' she said and kissed me. 'You're just a zombie slave.'

~

Aparna Di had been knocking on the door for quite some time now, I could tell. Avantika woke me up and we scrambled for our clothes.

'So, finally you two are up?' said Aparna Di, waiting at the table for both of us. I glanced at the clock. We had been inside that room for four hours; it was already ten.

'Avantika?'

'Yes, Di?'

'Don't make it so obvious,' Di said and pulled Avantika's hair out from under her T-shirt. Avantika smiled shyly.

'I don't know what you see in my brother. You're so pretty. Both of you look awful together. You should find someone better looking,' said Aparna Di. 'Taller and smarter.'

'On account of sharing the same bloodline,' I said, 'you should be on my side. And I have dated pretty girls before her, too.'

'Deb,' Di answered, 'I have seen everyone you have dated. None of them come even close.'

'Thank you, Aparna Di,' Avantika said and flashed her middle finger at me.

'Whatever, I know I'm average and stuff. You don't have to rub it in my face,' I conceded.

'Aw! See, so cute,' Avantika said. 'I have never met a guy so nice. That's why I love you. He's really a nice guy, Aparna Di. Like that.' She snapped her fingers.

'As long as you're happy, Avantika,' Di said. 'If he doesn't keep you happy, I can set you up with someone else.'

'I will keep that in mind, Di,' Avantika said and they both laughed.

Di said it was late and we should eat. We nodded; we had been hungry and exhausted from the bus ride. The maid served us prodigious quantities and we did not say no. The food was great, and Di attributed it to the expensive yet fabulous cook they had hired.

'The food is awesome, Aparna Di,' Avantika said appreciatively.

'I know. I tell him that all the time.' Aparna Di pointed towards the cook and we chuckled. I ate till I was bursting at my seams.

'Hey, I have something for you. Just wait here,' Aparna Di said and disappeared inside her room. A little later, she came out with an envelope in her hand.

'Here,' she handed over an envelope to Avantika. 'A small gift from Arnab and me for the two of you. This is the first time you have come to Pune and you can't go empty-handed.'

'What? We do not need this . . . you don't have to,' Avantika said as she opened the envelope and her voice trailed away. 'Umm?'

'What is it?' I asked, bending over to see what Avantika's trembling hands were holding.

'Two tickets to Goa?' Avantika mumbled.

'She is just trying to buy you with these things,' I said. 'Not that I mind.' I took the bunch of papers from her hand; flight tickets and hotel reservation receipts of what was clearly a high-end resort.

'Thank you so much,' Avantika said and hugged Aparna Di, teary eyed.

'It is my pleasure, Avantika. And remember my offer. I know many guys—Arnab's friends—who are tall and dark and handsome, quite unlike my brother who's, like, the ugly duckling of our beautiful family.'

'Deb is tall, dark and . . .' Avantika said and her words dried up. It was like those English movies, in which the daughter brings home a good-for-nothing son-in-law and says to her grumpy father, 'I know, Dad . . . He is the one.' I did not know what to do but smile stupidly.

'I wouldn't say anything to that,' Aparna Di said.

Avantika and Di chatted for a little while in the dining room, and I watched the rerun of an old India vs Australia test match. I had dozed off when Avantika woke me up.

'I simply love your sister,' Avantika gushed.

'Yes, you made that pretty evident.' I yawned.

'I want to marry you,' she said.

'Because you love my sister?'

'Yes,' she said. 'I would have gotten my brother to marry her if she was younger and he was older.'

'If wishes were horses, beggars would ride.'

'You are calling me a beggar?'

'Not yet. You are still not in skimpy rags or anything.'

'Deb! Is there a time of day when you're not thinking about sex?'

'No. You?' I asked her.

'Next topic please,' she said.

'I won that argument. Can we kiss already?'

'Just because you win,' she said and kissed me. 'Who told her about Goa?'

'I did,' I said. 'But I didn't ask her to get us tickets. It was all her. Arnab has a lot of money to spare it seems.'

'I love you.'

We switched off the lights and walked to our room, trudging slowly, our stomachs full and aching. I flopped on the bed and she wrapped herself around me.

'Remember the first time we met?' she asked.

'Yes, when you thought I was dumb and ugly?' I mocked.

'I never thought we would end up like this,' she said and ran her hands through my hair.

'Neither did I. I never believed in fate or destiny before I met you. But you made me believe in those.' I flicked away the hair from the front of her eyes and tucked them behind her ears. 'Why else would you be with me?'

'Why not?'

'I was never the right guy. Moreover, you were the right girl for millions of guys out there, guys who are better than me. Girls like you don't fall in love with guys like me.'

She held my hand and said, 'Words. Deb, words. That is what you have and that is what a girl needs. After a few years, even if you are not as cute as you are right now, your words would still have the magic they do now. They would still make me feel beautiful and wanted. You are all I need, Deb.'

She was right; words bound us together and no matter how much time passed between us, we still knew what to say to make everything all right. We hugged, with tears in our eyes, and our hearts filled with love and with memories of yesterday and fond images of tomorrow.

The next day, we left for Goa.

7

'I can't believe you just did that,' I said, my tongue flailing in my mouth in its drunkenness; she was sloshed too, red eyed and dangerously uninhibited.

'I didn't do it alone!' said Avantika, as she almost stumbled over a stray dog that yelped and ran.

'But it was you. You initiated it!' I accused her.

We had just made out in a nightclub's warehouse. There is something in Goa that just makes you so sexually charged; it's in the air really. Moreover, if you're dating someone like Avantika, it's unlikely that you wouldn't make out everywhere that you go.

'He was looking!'

'Who?' she asked as we lay down on the beach, yards away from where the water washed up. It was three in the night and the beach was deserted; even the policemen who patrol the beaches to catch unsuspecting horny couples had called it a day, or a night.

'The bartender! He was LOOKING.'

'I don't give a damn . . . But did you like it?'

'Like hell!' I said. 'But how much did you pay him to open the warehouse for you? The bartender?'

'I kissed him!' she shrieked.

30

'What?'

'On the cheek!' exclaimed Avantika. 'Duh. Obviously.'

'Ah . . . fine,' I said. 'Worth it.'

'Totally,' she said and we lay on our backs. We looked up at the starlit sky and listened to the roar of waves. We were the only ones there. I could make out the Orion, the only constellation I knew; the headless-legless woman in a sari. I was clearly still high.

'Deb?' Avantika broke the silence.

'Yes?'

'Do you want to do it here?' She looked at me with those drunken eyes, and ran her fingers over my face. My answer was already in the affirmative; the drool confirmed it.

'I have heard it's dangerous. Goa police is pretty strict about it!' I said.

'Is that a yes or no?'

'When has that ever been a no?'

I pulled her by the neck . . . She broke out of my embrace and walked towards the water. My head still spun from the alcohol I had drunk and the weed I had smoked, both of which were rare occurrences. By the time I stood up, she was in knee-deep water. She turned and looked at me. Slowly, she slipped out of her top. Her sarong was wet and floated on the water; she got rid of them. Only her red innerwear separated her from nakedness. Avantika covered her breasts with her hands, looked away from me and walked deeper into the water. The water on her fair legs glistened under the moonlight. She kept walking away from me, inviting me, as my unsure wasted steps took me towards her. Her hair blew across her face and the moonlight reflected off her flawless, wet skin.

Her washboard abs, the flat stomach, the most tastefully shaped breasts. The milky white sculpted thighs and calves. I was losing my head. I cut through the water to get to her. She removed her hands from her breasts and put them around my neck. We walked further away from the shore. The lights on the beach were now at a distance where we could hardly see them. We were neck deep in the water. There was water all around us. We breathed heavily. Waves splashed water all around, and she looked even more seductive as small water droplets clung to her face, and her wet hair stuck on her shoulders. It was just the two of us in an open wide sea—water, moonlight and lust engulfed us. We kissed.

The Goa trip was fabulous beyond words. The nights under the starlit sky on the deserted beaches, walks along the shores, lying next to each other until the sun rose . . . till it set again, the kisses in the neck-deep water, the pastas I loved, the pastas she hated for having had too much of them, the stolen kisses everywhere, places we lay bare, the hired bike and unchartered hikes, my shorts, her sarongs, my favourite tunes and her loved songs, the late-night walks and the aimless talks, the holding of hands, the waking up to the morning bands, the pointless staring, the clubs, the cocktails and the music blaring, the churches, the shacks, the strangers, the vodka, the hangovers.

For two days, life had stood still. We fell in love again. We celebrated it.

8

The train journey from Goa to Delhi and back to our hostel was uneventful except for the huge fight we had over Kabir where I was being unreasonable, and we spent twenty-odd hours staring outside the grilled windows of our train.

The company we had done our internship with had offered both Kabir and Avantika jobs in the same department. It was a little hard for me to accept that the two of them would be working together after a year, and it drove me nuts.

Kabir had even asked if they could find a place in Mumbai to live in together later. Avantika said she would talk about it when the time came. She should have shot it down, there and then! And how could he ask something like that? He knew that Avantika was dating me. We slept that night without talking to each other. Train journeys are extremely romantic, but the fight had drained the romance out of it.

We had the most hectic semester staring right at our faces.

Things were a little easier for Avantika since she had better grades and she already had a job. I scrambled inside the class at the last second and looked for Avantika. I had overslept, but my body still wanted more.

'This class?' the strategic management professor grumbled.

'Yes, sir,' I said meekly. I looked for Avantika in the class.

'Firstly, you are late for the class! And then you can't find a seat to sit?' he growled. 'No attendance for you. You can leave if you want to.'

'Okay, sir.' I decided to stay and not piss off the professor any more.

'Sit anywhere and stop disturbing the class,' he said sternly.

I sat on the first bench and cursed myself. *Not the brightest start to a semester*, I thought. I still tried to spot Avantika from the corner of my eyes but I could not. I texted her and asked where she was.

Right behind you. Last bench.

I waited for the professor to write something on the board so that I could look back. Last bench . . . she sat right next to that son of a bitch, Kabir. She was laughing. Nice. Just perfect.

It was a terrible start to the semester. I had missed attendance and Avantika was sitting with the guy I hated the most. I texted her just to make sure she wasn't talking to him, and she replied in a single 'K' and it made me even more uncomfortable. The next few messages met with the same treatment. I stopped sending them, and I kept looking back at the two of them. I heard them laughing again. *Bastard*.

'You two,' the professor pointed at the last bench. The class looked at Avantika and Kabir.

'Get up,' he said.

They were still smiling.

'Can you please share the joke with us too?' he bellowed.

Avantika looked down, embarrassed, though I could tell that she was still smiling.

'Get out,' the professor said.

Kabir immediately collected his books, pushed back his

chair and left. Avantika followed. They were still laughing when they left the class.

'If anyone has any more jokes to share they can do that outside the class,' he said and got back to telling us about some consulting project of his. I sat there and tried to concentrate on what the professor was saying to keep my mind off what Kabir was doing with my girlfriend. Where would these two be? What would they be doing? I was being paranoid but I could not help it.

I could not shake the thought off my head. Time stopped. Five minutes seemed like fifty. The more I stared at the clock hung above the blackboard, the slower it moved.

I fiddled with my pen and fidgeted in my hair. It became hard to keep sitting in the class. The last few minutes of that lecture were the most painful ones I had ever been through.

I messaged her, asking her where she was. 'Room,' the reply came. I felt relieved and slowed down my steps as I entered the girls' hostel.

Room No. 203.

I opened the door to her room. I hadn't bothered to knock.

'Hey,' said Kabir, sitting on her bed, one leg crossed calmly over the other, at home in Avantika's room.

'Where's she?' I asked, wanting to throw my hardbound register in his face and smashing his skull open. *What the fuck are you doing here!*

'She has gone to the washroom,' he said as he flipped through Avantika's magazines. That bastard had made himself comfortable in Avantika's room. *How can he even touch the magazines that she touched!*

'Deb, did he ask for our roll numbers?' he asked.

'I didn't notice,' I said and went out into the corridor. I walked around the corridor and waited for her.

'Where the fuck were you?' I asked as soon as I spotted her.

'In the room,' she said casually.

'Get him out of here right now!'

'What? Why?' she asked.

'Because I am asking you to do so.'

'Don't be such a kid, Deb.'

'Just do it, Avantika.'

'Okay, I will do that,' she said, a little miffed.

I waited outside the room for him to leave and he walked out after a couple of minutes. I was being unreasonable but I could not bear the sight of that man. I hated him with every cell of my body.

'What was he doing here?' I asked her.

'Nothing. We were just talking,' she said.

'Here? Is this the only place you got? In the whole campus?'

'It is hot outside, Deb.'

'Did he suggest this place?'

'Yes, kind of.'

'Why didn't you say no?'

'Why should I?' she asked innocently.

'As if you don't know what he wants from you!'

'He doesn't. Why are you being so possessive?'

'Possessive? You bring a guy to your room and you expect me not to react?'

'Deb, what do you think he was doing here?'

'I don't know! You tell me!' I accused her.

'Deb, if you think I had some wrong intentions, I don't think we should have this conversation. Do you really think—?'

'I am not saying anything. But we fought over him just yesterday! Is that not a problem?'

'I trust you, Deb. You don't . . .'

'That is because I don't keep hanging around with random girls and get them to my room.'

'Kabir is a friend.'

'Raghav has never come to your room and he is a better friend of yours. Nor has Ravi or Kumod! Why him?'

'I am not talking about this,' she said and looked away.

'How convenient.'

I left and banged the door behind me. *She must be crying now*, I thought. And like every egotistical guy, I didn't go back. I acted like an asshole and I did not like it but I hated him more; I wanted to make that clear, once and for all.

9

I ran through the conversation again in my head. Kabir would have laughed at me if he got to know about our fight. She would not text me, I knew. I was wrong and she waited for me to make it right. I did not want to accept defeat so easily. I made my way to the on-campus Nescafé stall that sold instant coffee and extra-spicy, microwave-cooked Maggi. Shashank had called, I remembered.

'How was Goa?' he asked.

'It was okay,' I said; my voice did not match up to his enthusiasm.

'Something happened?'

'Not really. Just a little fight.'

Mittal walked beside us with plates of noodles in his hands. Mittal's first name was Ganesh, but he preferred to be called by his last name—he said the name Ganesh reduced his raw sex appeal. Which he had in plenty, and he was well aware of it.

'Two lovelorn Romeos. What's happening, ladies?' he asked.

Mittal was not anti-relationships. In fact, there wasn't a time in the year he wasn't seeing anyone but he always disregarded the need of them. It's just how you get laid, he used to say. He was, basically, anti-love.

'Heard you went to Goa? Got laid? With your girlfriend? Now that's new and exciting!' he mocked. 'Who goes to Goa with his girlfriend? What's the point? How much did you spend?'

'Aparna Di gifted the tickets,' I said.

'Oh . . . involvement of family . . . very interesting indeed! Did she also give you small socks for Debashish Junior and Avantika Junior?' He laughed out and suddenly shrieked, 'Look there!'

'What?'

'Where?'

'There.'

Mittal pointed at an exchange student, Catherine, who had come from Poland. She looked like a familiar porn star. Mittal's and my eyes followed her exaggerated curves until they disappeared behind a pillar.

Shashank was not in the least interested. Being in a relationship never stopped me from leering at other women from time to time; Shashank was untouched by this kind of debauchery. He was loyal. Shashank and Farah had been going around for five years now. There had been problems in their relationship but they were still going strong. Farah belonged to a devout Muslim family, although she couldn't care less, and there was no way either of the families would approve of their relationship.

'Shashank?' Mittal asked. 'If Catherine . . . is standing naked right in front of you and offers you a blow job, would you let her do that to you?'

Mittal knew what the answer would be, and had started smiling. He was mocking him, but he was also fascinated by Shashank's righteousness.

'Nope,' Shashank said. He knew how Mittal would keep selling the idea to him and smiled.

Mittal continued selling the blow job. 'Shashank! Catherine! Imagine her naked, her huge red lips, her mouth inviting you; she would suck it good. It will be the best blow job of your life! You would even get to come wherever you want to. Even on her pretty face! How can you turn that down . . . Farah would not even get to know! You do watch porn, don't you? This is hardly different.'

We both looked at Mittal, shocked, disgusted and a tiny bit turned on. He could be really gross if he wanted to. We really did not want him to describe a blow job.

'I still wouldn't do it. Not with her at least,' Shashank said and smiled at me.

'Which means you will fuck her mentally, but not physically? That is being such a hypocrite . . . Anyway, Deb, what about you?'

'I would do it,' I said. I did not want to come across as a wimp. I don't know whether I was being a hypocrite, or I was just angry at Avantika.

'Me too!' Mittal said and laughed. 'In fact, I am ready to pay for it too!'

'Oh . . . good that you added the last part and gave some respect to her,' I said.

'She deserves it, Deb, she deserves it. Shashank? Are you done with the chapter?'

Shashank was our saviour in class. He was a year or two younger than we were, and the only sincere one amongst us. He was departmental rank two and it was effortless for him, and we loved it when he kicked butt of the snobbish kids who slogged throughout the semester, took notes, ran after professors and submitted their assignments on time.

Shashank did not look twenty-three and still looked like a schoolchild; his looks were in stark contrast to the person he was. Responsible, straight-thinking and very composed.

'Read it yourself. It's not that tough,' he said to us.

'What? Are you crazy? We will not get it. Just read it and tell us what it is all about!' Mittal said.

Shashank narrated the case for the next class. I was only half listening and Mittal had to slap my head a few times to make me concentrate. We rushed to the class minutes before it started. As a reflex, I ran my eyes through the crowd and looked for Avantika until I realized that I was not supposed to do so. We were in the middle of a fight.

The three of us found a place for us to sit. Avantika was sitting in the first row and furiously making notes. Kabir sat close by, just a girl between them, and they talked once or twice every few minutes. I suppressed the urge to text her. It was hard to see her even talking to him. I could not even fathom why she was . . . I mean she knew that I would be watching her in class. She should have stayed away from him. It just made me sick now.

'Should we get him beaten up?' Mittal whispered in my ear, smilingly.

'Shut up, man . . .'

'See, that is why I say—get only so close to a girl that she warms you, not burns you up!' he said seriously. 'You get the pun, right? Warm is equal to sex? Burn is equal to jealousy? Brilliant, right?'

'Shut up . . .'

'If you have a problem with him, why don't you go and talk to her?' said Shashank, concerned.

'I will not. It is the same every time. She will put forth some big words like trust and love, and I will lose the conversation again. Why should it be me always? Why can't she lose the argument sometimes?'

'Guys are supposed to take the initiative, that is how it works,' Shashank said.

'That is how my dick works too. Suck it,' Mittal said. 'This is because we pamper girls! Stop pampering them and lower their expectations. They will be out of excuses to cry. It's as simple as that.'

'SILENCE!' the brand management professor bellowed. 'The students who haven't submitted the assignment need to see me after the class.'

The moment he said it, I assumed that I had to go. I looked at these two to see if they had submitted it. They shook their heads and we smiled because not only did we miss the deadline, we did not even know about the assignment at all. The class ended and the professor shouted out the names of the students who had not submitted the assignment. My name wasn't on the list. Mittal and Shashank looked at me as if they had caught me in a threesome with their sisters; I had violated the bro code; I had submitted an assignment when they hadn't, and in the universe bound together with the tenuous ties between brothers, between comrades, this was unacceptable.

'Avantika,' I explained.

They let out a collective sigh.

'If you two are fighting, can I ask her out? I really need someone to do my assignments too,' Mittal smirked.

'Lucky dog . . .' Shashank said. 'That is why I said there are some places girls take the initiative, where you never would.'

'Oh, Shashank, stop bullshitting! We don't need such statements from a guy who even takes the initiative to wash his girl's clothes.'

'I just picked up laundry once,' he said in his defence.

'As if you wouldn't have washed them too, had she asked! You would have washed her maid's clothes too, if given the chance,' he grumbled.

'Anyway, Deb, the fight ends?' Shashank asked.

'I don't know,' I said.

What does one do when one's girlfriend is like the sweetest little thing ever? You just feel that you are the stupidest guy in the whole world. I was the stupidest guy with the sweetest girl one could ever have.

10

She left the class and Kabir left closely behind. Not the prettiest of scenes for me, but I had the first right on her, so I brushed Kabir aside and asked her if we could talk. Kabir slinked away. I followed her to the coffee shop inside our college and we started to talk.

'Thank you,' I said.

'For what?' she asked. The coffee froth perched playfully on her pink lips. She licked it away.

'For the assignment,' I said, apologetically.

'You never thanked me before for it,' she said, trying hard not to show that she was smiling.

'We never fought this bad before . . . I guess.'

'It is okay, baby,' she said, ran her palm over my cheek. Her one touch and I was her puppy again.

'I am sorry.'

'It is fine,' she said. She drank her coffee in silence. 'Come,' and led me by her hand to our hostel and then to her room.

'So?' I asked after we reached her room. 'What?'

'What what?' she said.

'I mean why your room?'

'. . . because unlike some people I think people do a lot more than just kiss each other all over behind a closed

44

door. They can discuss corporate finance too, you know,' she explained.

'I get your point. It is just that I am not comfortable. I'm a little insecure. Who wouldn't be if he is dating a stunner like you?'

'That's sweet. But I love you, Deb. Why don't you understand that? Why do you still doubt me?'

'It is not as if I doubt you. It is just that I do not want Kabir to feel that he has a chance with you. I know this is silly, but I can't help it.'

'I know, baby,' she said and rubbed her nose on my neck.

'Would you not feel bad if I hang around with Malini?'

'Not at all, Deb. I trust you. I really do. I do not trust her, but that is another thing. I know you would always be with me,' she said and pecked me on my cheek.

'I always will.'

'Now go away from my room. I got to study. Go and meet your Malini,' she said and pushed me out. I scratched my head as I stood outside her room.

Why bring me all the way to your room and not make out? What happened to the concept of patch-up sex! Kids these days!

11

Mittal shouted as soon as he saw me in the corridor, 'Had sex and solved everything?'

Everybody turned and looked at him. I ground my teeth and widened my eyes to make him shut up. He always made us look like some sex-obsessed group in college.

'What happened?' Shashank asked.

'Nothing much . . . We talked and everything is normal.'

'What?' Mittal exclaimed as he lit a cigarette. 'You talked? You were in her room. Why didn't you just sleep with her? That is how you tell the girl is still yours. You sleep with her and tell the whole world about it. It's a simple two-step process.'

'I don't have to do that,' I said. 'No, thank you.' I turned down his cigarette.

'Have a cigarette, dude . . . See these are just like girls. Put on to your lips, it feels great. A few minutes later, it just burns out. Then you need another one! And another one. That is how girls are. You fall in love with them and slowly, it becomes a habit. Navy cut one day, Marlboro the other. You cannot kick the habit. But you feel good about it every time you puff one! Or fuck one!'

'Where does he get such ideas from?' Shashank asked.

'I wish I knew,' I said.

'You know it is so sad that both my friends suck so much. Life is beyond love, guys. It is beyond running after girlfriends, beyond buying them gifts when you would rather buy stuff for yourself and aligning your life according to them. Shashank, when was the last time you went out with a girl who was not Farah? Three years?'

'Four,' he replied.

'See? How do you know she is the one for you when you don't even consider other girls?'

'See, that is where you are wrong, Mittal. I don't feel the need. I just want to be with her,' Shashank said. He always talked beyond his age and his looks, almost like a phoney god-man.

'You are wimps. Both of you! You are scared. You are scared that you are not men enough to get more than what you already have. Where's the ambition? Where's the fire?'

'I still agree with what Shashank said. I don't feel the need,' I said.

'I am not asking you fuckers to start sleeping around with everything that moves on two legs and has breasts,' Mittal defended himself.

'Then what do you want us to do?' I asked.

'Just go out! Have some fun and give yourself a friggin' chance!' Mittal blabbered.

'I think we really need to do the marketing assignment now. That's where we should channel all our ambition and fire towards,' Shashank said and I nodded.

Mittal flapped opened the laptop irritably. He was pissed that we were unmoved. He desperately wanted us to sleep around. Why? We never knew. It is a guy thing, I guess. If a friend gets laid, it's like you getting laid; vicarious promiscuity.

We had hardly started studying when Mittal's phone beeped and he left the room. Mittal never took those calls in front of us. Shashank and I had tried but never succeeded in finding out who the mysterious girl was ... Or the mysterious girls ...

'Who do you think it is?' I looked at Shashank. He shook his head and got back to his books.

Mittal had never formally introduced us to any of the girls he went out or slept with. Every few days, a new hot girl would leave his hostel room with her hair ruffled, lipstick smudged and with love bites on her neck, but he never let us talk to anyone. It was creepy.

'I don't want you guys to be friends with any of the girls I go out with,' he had once said.

'Why?' I had asked.

'I don't want to get caught. I lie to them all the time. I don't want them calling you and asking about me! Naah! I can't let that happen,' he had explained.

He had a point there. Your lies should always be unverifiable. Anyway, we often suspected that Mittal was hiding something. We expected that one fine day, he would break down in front of us and would say something like, 'I was dumped by this girl five years ago and since then all I have been trying to do is to get back with her. I attempted suicide twice.' Nothing of this sort ever happened. Not even close. Over the past twelve months, we had seen more than a dozen girls leave that fated hostel room, violated and smiling.

'I don't think I can study any more,' I said.

'You're leaving the rest of it?' Shashank asked.

'Yep,' I said and shut down my laptop. He did the same. Shashank was in bad company. Mittal and I knew that without our unholy influence on him, Shashank would have topped every goddamned exam in MDI, but we loved him too much to lose him to books and marks. We could lose him to blow jobs from porn stars from Poland, but definitely not to *Free Market Economics.*

'Didn't college get over too soon?' Shashank said.

'Seriously, it has been a year and it hardly feels like it. It should have lasted four years. At least!'

'Yea, we wish,' he said wistfully. 'I just hope Farah gets placed in the same city as I.'

'Hmm . . . yeah.'

'So what have you and Avantika thought?'

'As in?'

'Are you getting married?'

'Eventually. In a few years, maybe. I mean we intend to. Her parents would object but you know the equation there.'

'Your parents?'

'They wouldn't be too happy about it. But I guess, if I push them, they would not say no. After all there are so many love marriages around, aren't there?'

'Yes.'

'Hmm . . . so you and Farah?'

'We can't get married,' he sighed. 'Umm . . . you know.'

Though he had done his graduation from Delhi and that is where he had met Farah, Shashank belonged to a powerful industrial family based in Meerut.

'My family wouldn't let me marry Farah.'

'The Muslim factor?' I asked. They had been together for a few years now, and they had broken up a few times because they knew, one day, they would have to break up. But it's easier said than done.

'Yes.'

'Hmm . . . so, when are you going to break up with her? You have to do it soon, man,' I asked, not sure whether I should be asking the question.

'I know . . . but then, it's so hard not to be with each other,' said Shashank, barely hiding his sadness.

Mittal and I had asked him more than a few times to end his relationship with Farah and make it easier for both of them. He tried but he could never do it. He was irrevocably in love with her. We realized that Mittal had overheard our conversation when he rudely interrupted it.

'You guys are such girls! Twenty-three and you want to get married?' Mittal said. 'It is a long way off . . . who knows what will happen in six years! By the way, assignment? Where is that going?'

'It is done with,' I said.

'Great. I am going to the gym. See you in an hour,' he said, picked up his gym bag and left. Mittal was a gym freak, and never missed a day. Not even between exams, and it showed. One could mistake his biceps for tiny footballs. He used to walk shirtless in the corridors, his hard, well-defined chest in full view, and enjoy the admiring smiles of both the sexes.

'Deb, catch you later,' Shashank said as he stuffed his laptop inside his bag.

'Farah?'

'Yes. It is her birthday tomorrow. So I have to buy something for her.'

'You have decided what to get for her?'

'I was thinking of getting her a ring . . . but I don't want to give her the wrong idea,' he said and left.

I wanted to be sad about it, but I was smiling that I had no wrong ideas to be worried about. The whole idea of Avantika and me, together for life, was comforting. However, before it would happen, it would be a long and tiring fight to convince our parents and relatives. Was I ready? I thought so. I wanted her to be there for me.

Shashank and Farah—I had hardly imagined them without each other. To think that they would not be together was strange. It was a creepy thought to think they would be with different people. Deb and Avantika? With different people? That felt downright sick. Love makes you so dependent. To imagine my life without Avantika was a ridiculous thought.

I revised the chapter.

12

Avantika and I had our differences, but that's what made us special. Avantika had always been an ambitious girl, and toiled hard to get what she wanted. She worked hard to secure herself from any more heartbreaks or disappointments. Her previous relationships had been total disasters that saw her spiralling down into a haze of alcohol and drugs for a couple of years. She had been to a series of rehabilitation centres but she had run away and had almost destroyed herself when, at last, she found a spiritual connection with Spirit of Living and Sri Guru. She has not touched drugs since. She had her relapses and slipped into depression now and then. My promises of forever used to make it all right. It pained me to see her in pain, and it made me sick when I could not make it better.

My life was a lot different. I had always been laid-back and my relationships had been a joke. I had never felt love before I met Avantika; my relationships had always been a bag full of sweetened lies, meaningless dates and cards with someone else's words on them.

Our relationship was like a fairy tale, scripted, and it was scary to think how good we made each other feel. The princess kisses the frog; the frog remains a frog; the princess still decides to dump all princes and stay with the frog; she even sleeps with the frog. It was just so biased that one would believe the frog scripted it.

'Where is Kabir?' I mocked her as I sat next to her.

'Shut up. He is working on the case study.'

'Case study?'

'The Mahindra one? The one you refused saying that it was bullshit?'

'You are still working on it? Who else is in the team?'

'Just the two of us.'

'Oh . . . just you two?' I winked.

'Yeah . . . now start the taunts!'

'So when do you have to send it?'

'Today.'

'Oh . . . and what if you get selected?'

'We will have to go to Mumbai and present the case. IIT Mumbai, their fest is coming up and they—'

'Mumbai? You two?' *What the fuck?*

'Yes. Oh, don't start it again,' she said and rolled her eyes.

'No, I won't, but just a little uncomfortable. Never mind, I too will send the case study, with Malini. She is intelligent and stuff,' I smirked.

'Oh . . . you won't work with me, but you will work with her, huh?' She smiled.

'Why not? If you can work with Kabir, I can work with Malini!'

'No, I will be happy if you do. At least you will do something,' she said, patted my back and concentrated on the class.

Mumbai? With Kabir? Alone? This cannot be!

I made up my mind to start working on the case study though I knew I would not stand a chance, not even if Malini agreed to work with me, which I was sure she wouldn't.

'So?' I asked Avantika. 'What all has to be put in the presentation?'

Avantika started to tell me about what she and Kabir had done. I had already given up before even starting. I could not possibly match what they had done or even come close.

'You did all that?' I asked, shocked at how much detail they had put into the presentation. 'How long have you been working on this?'

'A few days,' said Avantika proudly.

'. . . and when is the deadline?'

'Tonight!' she said.

Fuck it. It did not matter any more . . . there was no way I could have made that presentation. We left the class. Avantika looked as if in a hurry and I asked her where she was running to.

'I have to go meet Kabir and add a few things,' she said.

'Add? More?'

'Whatever. Aren't you doing it? With Malini?' She smiled at me.

'Fuck you.'

'Later. I am busy tonight,' she said and winked. I saw her leave and meet Kabir in the mess. *That asshole.*

Maybe, I needed to make this crazy presentation. But who would help me out? Malini? I was the only guy in class she ever talked to, but we were not, like, friends. I could have made the presentation with Shashank, but that wouldn't have served the purpose.

13

I toyed with the idea of teaming up with Malini for quite some time, but the fear of rejection kept me from talking to her. Of what I knew of her, she was a sharp and intelligent girl who could help me out if she wanted. Our past conversations had been pleasant but not friendly, so I didn't know what to expect. *There is no harm in trying*, I told myself. So that afternoon, I followed Malini as she made her way to her hostel room.

'MALINI,' I called her name aloud.

'Yes?' said Malini, her accent still very pronounced.

Malini had done the last few years of her high school and her undergraduate studies in Canada, and had come back with a heavy accent, an adjustment problem that people mistook as attitude and a bold dressing sense. Our college being one of overachievers and nerds, our classmates never approved of what she wore sometimes, but she wasn't looking for approval. Some people thought Malini was slutty—probably because they were jealous of how hot she was or that she was out of their league—but she had never been involved with anyone in college. The red streaks in her hair didn't help either. With her corpse-white complexion, and a sculpted body hardened by hours of jogging in the college campus, she looked like a diminutive model for a luxury brand. Initially, many people had mistaken her for an exchange student. Long story short, she was hot stuff.

'There is this case study competition in Mumbai. It is pretty interesting and I was wondering . . .'

'I have read it,' she interrupted.

'Oh . . . nice . . . I have started working on it . . . and it is almost finished . . . I just need a team member—'

'Almost finished it?' She started to walk away from me, her legs making an eight on the mess floor.

'Yes, almost.'

'Then why do you need me?'

'It is a team of two. And you know, having a girl in the team helps,' I said and smiled. People had told me in the past that I did not look ugly when I smiled and that my dimple made up for my other ape-like features. I hoped it would work.

'Having a girl helps? That's chauvinistic and sexist.' She frowned.

'Umm . . . err . . .'

'Anyway, you have finished it?'

'To be honest, I haven't started.' I smiled sheepishly.

'That is what I thought.' She laughed, almost like a villainous smirk, not really a laugh, but a smirk and a broad smile in an odd composition. 'So you want to work on it together?'

'Precisely.'

'See you at nine. Mess?'

I nodded and she left.

~

Moments later, I entered my hostel room and found Mittal sprawled on my bed; he was smiling. I was sure he had seen me talk to Malini, his *dream* girl, the girl he had always wanted to lay his hands on; but Malini was unapproachable and ruthless and even Mittal's charms could never break her.

'Giving yourself a chance?' asked Mittal.

'What?'

'Remember I told you? Other girls? Fuck, do you even listen to what I say? You will be a lot wiser if you just listen to me.'

'What other girls? Malini? No!'

'No? What was that then? You and her? Middle of the mess? You guys were smiling like long-lost friends.'

'We are just working on a case study together,' I said.

'Case study? YOU?'

'Yes.'

'Don't make me laugh, man,' he said and looked at me. I maintained the deadpan expression. 'What bullshit, Deb?' He looked betrayed.

'Yes . . .'

'What is the deal, man?' he asked me in disbelief.

'Nothing. Avantika is participating with Kabir. So, I thought I would participate too.'

He looked at me with widened eyes and said, 'Deb, you know that you are psychologically imbalanced, right? You are doing a case study because she is doing the same with Kabir? That self-satisfied asshole.'

'Not really.'

'Fuck you. Why are you being so possessive? If she wants to be with him, let her! You cannot keep sticking to her all the time. This is so . . . disgusting. You disappoint me!' he exclaimed.

'It is not that, I just want to be around her,' I defended myself.

'It's exactly that. You just don't trust your girlfriend.'

'I do.'

'Why Malini then? Why not some guy? Shashank? He would do a much better job of it.'

'It is something between Avantika and me. You don't need to know anything.'

Mittal rolled his eyes. 'Whatever. Anyway, what did Malini say?' he asked.

'She said yes,' I said.

'She did? I thought she had loads of attitude—'

'Nah, she is sweet.'

'I think she has a thing for you,' said Mittal scornfully.

'I don't think so.'

My phone beeped and vibrated in my pocket. It was Malini and she wanted to meet me. It was three hours too early. As I left the room, Mittal's words kept ringing in my head. Maybe, I did not trust Avantika. It had been three years now. I knew she would never do anything that would hurt me. But all said and done, I still did not like Kabir hanging around my girlfriend. She was mine, and I wanted to keep it that way. I wasn't ready to lose her to anyone, especially that smug bastard.

14

Malini's room was spotlessly clean like Avantika's room was, but still it looked different. The lights were dim and yellow; there were cushions and beanbags that crowded her room. It really looked like a gypsy had settled down. I liked her room. It was different from the other rooms of the hostel that were always crowded with big management books and magazines about marketing and finance, reminders of our fate as boring management graduates.

'I read the case,' said Malini, sitting cross-legged on her bed. She wore a nightdress that ended midway over her thighs. *There is no harm in looking*, I told myself.

'Aren't we like three hours too early?'

'I didn't feel sleepy enough, so I read it,' she answered.

'So, shall we start?' she asked.

'Sure,' I said.

'Should we study here? Or the library?' she asked.

'Here,' I said. I swear to God my intentions were innocent. I know I had been staring at her ever since I entered her room, but I had no shady intentions. I was there just for revenge. I sat on her bed beside her. I felt sorry for my outburst with Avantika when I had found Kabir in her room. They were innocent, and so was I. Malini handed over the papers that I had to study from; they were marked and underlined and stuck with tiny post-it notes. We had just started to study when she broke the silence.

'Want something?' she asked.

'As in?'

'Vodka, gin, whisky?' she asked. She got up from where she sat and pulled out a mini freezer from below her bed. It was plugged into a spike which was plugged in with about a dozen plugs—a disaster waiting to happen.

'Anything?' she asked and dangled a mini bottle of vodka.

'Umm . . . no,' I said. 'I'm good.'

'Fine,' she said and made herself a drink—a lot of vodka with a hint of Sprite. I had never seen anyone stock alcohol in the hostel rooms, definitely not in a mini fridge. I didn't know whether I was supposed to be impressed or intimidated.

'Let's start. I will just write the brief overview of the case; you start with the impact,' she said, and sipped on her drink. We started to work on our slides. I tried to concentrate but I kept looking at her, stealing glances as she gulped her drink in three swallows. She made another one for herself. She raised the glass in the air to ask me if I needed one, and I refused.

'Done?' she asked after about an hour.

'Not really,' I said. 'It's tougher than I expected.'

She was already on her third drink. 'I need another one,' said Malini. 'How many hours are we left with?' she asked flapping down her laptop.

'Seven to go.'

'We can take a break then.' She kept the laptop aside and finished her drink in a rather manly gulp. 'So, Deb, isn't Avantika participating in this one?'

'She is.'

'But not with you?'

'With Kabir.'

She smiled as if she knew what I was trying to achieve. 'You guys are pretty serious about each other, right?'

'You can say so,' I said. It always bothered me to tell pretty girls that I was taken, but it was a small price to pay to be with someone as great as Avantika.

'Sweet,' she said. I could sense the sarcasm in her voice. 'How long has it been for the two of you?' she asked and her phone rang. 'Wait a minute.'

She left the room. I logged into Facebook and waited for her to come back. Ten minutes. Twenty minutes. She was still on her phone call.

'Hey,' I called up Avantika.

'What's up? Are you out somewhere? I went to your room too, but you weren't there.'

'I am in Malini's room. The case study thing,' I said.

'You were serious about it? You're already in her room? Nice moves, boyfriend!' she mocked and chuckled. *Can't she just be jealous and quit the competition so that I can do the same?*

'And where are you?'

'I am in the library, with Kabir. LIBRARY. NOT MY ROOM. *Now* who is the culprit?' she mocked.

'I am sorry for that. Now can you please shut up about it?'

'If you insist. So how is the presentation shaping up?' she asked.

'Hey, I am sorry. I just had to take that call,' Malini said as she entered the room. 'Let's get started.'

'It is going fine. Will catch you later,' I whispered into the phone and disconnected the line.

'Talking to Avantika?' asked Malini, her eyes bloodshot and a silly smile on her face. She had downed half a bottle of vodka and I was still standing straight; that's badass. She picked up the laptop and started to tap furiously on it. She did not talk too much. For the next four hours, she concentrated on the work like a sniper, often prodding me to work harder. She looked a little upset but I could not ask her why. We were not even friends so I let her be.

'Done?' she asked as she scrolled through the entire thirty-eight slides.

'I think so.'

'Wait.' She tweaked the background of the slides and asked, 'Now?'

'Better.'

'Wait then.' She downloaded another background option and changed it. 'Now?'

'It's all the same to me. Aesthetics isn't my strongest suit.'

'Now we are done,' she attached the file to the mail and asked me for the mail ID at which we had to send the file. She typed it down and we shared a nervous smile before she hit the send button. It was certainly a feat for me; six hours and I had not moved an inch from where I was sitting. Avantika would be so proud to hear that.

'Calls for a drink?' she asked.

'Sure. Haven't you had enough?'

'When I pass out, that's when I say I have had enough,' said Malini with a melancholic smile.

No bad intentions still, I was genuinely happy. I wanted to call up Avantika and ask how much they had done.

'Vodka?' she asked.

'Yep,' I said.

She had been gulping it neat (almost) so I thought it would be girlish of me to ask for something to accompany mine.

'You drink a lot, do you?' I asked since I wasn't much of a drinker.

'I used to drink in Toronto. I have reduced now,' she said and smiled at me.

'By the way, thank you for the help.'

'Thank you? It is our case study.' She gulped down her drink like it was water.

'True,' I said and gulped mine. The vodka burnt my throat, my stomach and my face distorted. It was horrible.

'Too strong?' she asked.

'Understatement,' I said, the taste still singed my tongue. 'Molten fire.'

'You are a kid,' she said.

'Really? Don't throw me a challenge!' I said playfully, hoping that she wouldn't but she did and I lost. After the fifth shot, which tasted much better than the previous four since my taste buds had died, I was positively drunk and a little pukey. My stomach started to retch and I sat there, unmoving, scared that I would upset the balance if I got up and might puke all over her bed sheet.

I sat there, listening to her talk. Malini said she missed Canada a lot and that she did not like her time in India and could not wait to go back to Toronto. She said something about a boyfriend in Canada but I only remember his name—Samarth.

'I don't want to talk about him,' said Malini, teary eyed, though I had not yet said a word. 'Thank you. I think we should sleep now. This is getting to my head.' She pointed to the glass in her hand.

'Yes. We have worked too hard for a day. I think I am a little drunk too.' The world spun every time I blinked.

'A little drunk?'

'Okay—a lot! I think I should go,' I said and got up. My stomach grumbled in anger.

'Stay,' said Malini. I saw pearls of tears at the edges of her eyes. I knew she was about to cry. She added immediately, 'No . . . you should go.'

'I can stay if you want me to.'

I felt sorry for her. No matter how drunk I was, I realized that Malini was lonely out here. And her relationship problems weren't helping her either.

'You have done enough, Deb. Thank you. Bye,' she said and closed the door on my face.

I could still hear her crying and sniffing behind the door. Malini had always been a strange girl. She never talked to any of our classmates and we usually thought she was snotty and snobbish. After all, she drove a sparkling Audi Q7 and that in itself is intimidating. Everybody thought twice before talking to her.

I staggered straight to the washroom and vomited my intestines in the sink. Just before I deposited my wasted body on to my mattress, my phone beeped and it was a text from Malini.

Felt good today. Thank you. I hope we did well. Good night.

15

The phone had been ringing for quite some time now. My eyes were closed shut and I was still drunk.

'Sleeping?' asked Avantika groggily. 'You are done?'

'Yes. We sent it an hour ago,' I said. I smelled of dead rats in my mouth. 'So tired.'

'I wish you could come over,' said Avantika.

'Hmm.' I didn't know if I wanted to be with her; my head was still spinning and I felt dehydrated and sick.

At MDI, guys weren't allowed in the girls' hostel beyond eleven in the night, though girls could be in the boys' hostel at any time, but they preferred not to be among hairy, shirtless, stinking guys in boxers.

'I wish you were next to me,' said Avantika.

'Why do you think I want anything different?' I asked, half-heartedly.

'Come over then,' she said.

'But . . .'

'Nobody will know.'

'But—'

'Yes, you are right,' said Avantika, dejected. It was risky but no one ever really got caught.

'I will come.'

'But what if—'

'No one will know, Avantika. I will dash in and leave in the morning. What say?'

'It is a little risky.'

'When did we stop taking risks?' I asked her. 'And it's not the first time we are doing this.'

'Just don't get caught,' she said and cut the line.

I trudged to the washroom, washed my face and brushed my teeth vigorously. My head still hurt and I could still not keep my eyes open. I crossed the well-lit corridor that led to the girls' hostel with drunk, unsure steps. If I were to get caught, it would be a huge waste. I called Avantika when I was about ten paces from her room. I could already smell her in the air.

'Clear?' I whispered.

'Wait.' I stood at the foot of the stairs waiting for her to give a go. 'Now!' she said.

I made a mad dash up the stairs and then a left and then a right. I ran right into her room and she closed the door behind her. I panted as I got to her room.

'Not that tough, eh?' she asked.

'Not really.' I smiled.

She held my dangling hand and tugged at it, while I came close. 'So, why are you here? Girls' hostel? So late in the night, it's not allowed, is it?'

She was inches away from me and I could feel her breath through my shirt. Anything that was forbidden, like the boss's chambers, conference rooms, deserted beaches, parked cars on a deserted road . . . all this got Avantika's hormones running. So did mine.

'I missed you,' I said as she let her lips hover around mine.

'Did you drink?' she asked. 'You smell horrible.'

'Kind of.'

'With?' she asked.

'Malini. Just one drink. She insisted that we should celebrate.'

'But you were in her room all day? Weren't you? Where did you drink?'

'She has tiny vodka bottles stashed under her bed. She has a functional mini bar beneath her bed.'

'Do you like her?' she asked.

'She is nice.'

'Nice? Nice?' She pressed a love bite from a few days before which still pained.

'DON'T DO THAT. I was kidding!'

She let it go and instead, planted her lips on my neck, and started to suck on it. She bit, and bit hard enough to leave a mark.

'Now that would leave a hickey,' I said as soon as she left me. I inspected it in the mirror; it was red and would soon turn purple.

'I want it to,' she said. 'I want a stamp on you that says you are *mine*.'

'I don't mind it. It's good for my ego that someone like you deigns to give someone like me love bites. It just proves that I'm sleeping with the most desirable girl on campus,' I responded. 'I should be giving you one too. You know, to tell Kabir that you are mine?'

'I tell him that often. And you shouldn't worry about him,' said Avantika.

'And you shouldn't worry about her,' I said.

She slipped away from my grasp and sat on her bed, biting her nails and looking at her lap.

'Aww . . . what happened, baby?'

'Nothing,' she said.

'Just say it.'

'It's nothing. I just want you to know that I really need you. I want you to be around.'

'I will be. But why do you say that today?' I asked.

'Deb, you are here now. But tomorrow you might find someone. Someone better than me ... and when that happens, I don't want to cling on to you.'

'You are talking nonsense, Avantika,' I protested.

'Just keep me around. I will be happy to see you happy,' she said. She looked like a hurt puppy but I basked in the glory of being wanted and loved.

'Avantika, I would never find anyone who is as beautiful, as sweet, or as funny as you are. I love you and that is never going to change. You taught me what love is. Leaving you would mean unlearning all that, and I do not want to do that. I cannot do that. You are a part of me now and I cannot let you go. Not even if I want to. You are the only thing I want. You are the only thing I need.'

I sat beside her and she clung to me. I felt lucky that I was around her and that she loved me. I had also imagined how life would be without her. It was barren, loveless and purposeless.

16

'Deb! Saw the mail?' Avantika shouted from a distance. Morning classes were the worst, especially the ones where professors took it as a personal insult if students didn't turn up on time.

'What mail?' I asked groggily. I dumped shreds of half-cooked omelettes on my plate and poured ketchup all over it to make it taste better.

'Yours is chosen!' she shrieked.

'Huh?'

'Such a lame reaction!'

'The Mumbai thing? The case study? And you?' I asked, not in the least interested. It had been more than a week since we had sent those case studies and I had completely forgotten about it since I had not fancied my chances.

'No,' said Avantika. I searched for disappointment on her face but couldn't find any. 'But you go and win it for me.'

'What? I am not going,' I said.

'Why not? You worked hard for it! You should go.'

'Worked hard?' I said. 'I just worked on it for a few hours. I only did it to make you jealous, and now that it's done I no longer care.'

'Don't bullshit me, Deb. For the first time, you did something constructive, don't let it go,' grumbled Avantika.

'What do you mean?' I got slightly pissed off at her statement, though she was right.

'You know what I meant, Deb; you got to take charge some time. You have to be a little serious about things. You are more intelligent and smarter than many people around, and you should realize that you can make a difference. Do something that will make me proud.'

'Make you proud? Didn't I just get through a competition that you didn't?'

'You have to see this through. You can't back out now,' said Avantika.

'Why do you always have to make so much sense?'

'I was just born smart,' she said, then smiled and held my hand, her chin upturned in pride.

Kabir was furious that they could not get through. 'How did he get through?' Kabir had asked Avantika.

~

'So are you going?' asked Shashank, scared and concerned.

'Obviously, he is! You never know what might happen there, Deb. If anything happens on a vacation, it doesn't count as cheating,' Mittal said.

'I don't want anything to happen,' I said.

'Idea!' Mittal said. 'Why don't you go to Goa again? With Malini? This time the trip might actually mean something. Imagine, man ... both of you are drunk and Malini asks you to rub suntan lotion on her back. Is there anything else you could possibly want?' he said, already drooling.

'That only happens in *American Pie* movies. And I don't want to go.'

'Don't tell me it's because you will miss Avantika,' Mittal mocked.

'Shut up, man,' Shashank said.

'I feel she gets a little insecure when I am around others,' I said.

'So what? That shouldn't stop you,' Mittal said disgustingly. 'She should understand; isn't that what relationships are all about? Both of you need to stop being Siamese twins.'

'Will you ever stop being an asshole?' Shashank said irritably.

'Me? Asshole? That is what *you* guys are! Get a life,' he smirked and was about to add on when his phone rang loudly. He flashed a middle finger at us and left the room.

'Deb, but I think you should go,' Shashank said. 'I talked to Avantika and she was excited about it! Don't disappoint her.'

'I know . . .'

'Anyway, you didn't mail me the case study that you sent?'

'I will do it right now,' I said and opened my laptop.

'But why didn't you ask me to work on it?' He seemed pissed.

'Because you don't have boobs and I wanted someone who could make her jealous,' I said. 'She has always been bothered about Malini.'

Shashank laughed. He started to look through the presentation, pausing at the ones with pie charts and bar graphs, and was genuinely impressed. I felt good about myself, and I now saw what Avantika was trying to tell me. It feels good to have a boyfriend who is not worthless.

17

I called Malini for the hundredth time that day. Having made up my mind to go to Mumbai, I wanted to start preparing, and see this competition through to its end. If not for anything else but to prove to Kabir, the ass of the highest order, that he can shove his superiority complex up his behind.

Finally, she picked up.

'Where are you?' I asked, almost angrily.

'Why do you care, man?' She sounded drunk and her Canadian accent was even heavier. 'What's up, man?'

Her ghetto-style language always somewhat caught me off guard. The extensive usage of 'fuck it' and 'man' took some time for me to get used to.

'Nothing much, Malini. Just wanted to tell you that our case study has been selected and we can go to Mumbai to fight for the top spots.'

'And what about your girl's?'

'They didn't get through,' I said.

'Are we really that good?' said Malini, her tongue failing her.

'Maybe! You did most of it, so you definitely are good. So we are going?' I asked her.

'No.'

'Why? We worked hard for it! We have a fair chance of winning this.'

'See, Deb, you wanted to go because she was going with that fuck-all prick. So, it doesn't make sense to go now,' she said.

'But we worked hard for it,' I argued.

'I don't care about it. Neither do you. So just fuck it.' She laughed aloud. 'I'm sure it's not you but your girlfriend talking. She wants you to go, doesn't she?'

'Does it matter?'

'Maybe.'

~

'Packed everything?' Avantika asked. 'Toothpaste? Foam? Slippers? Did you check everything on the list I made?'

'Yes, baby. How many times will you ask?'

'It's just that . . .' she choked. 'We have never been away for so long, so it feels a little strange.'

'Aww!' I hugged her. 'Don't cry.'

'I can't help it,' she said.

'Go ahead. You look cute when you cry.'

'Just go and win. Don't let me down,' she said. The taxi honked and reached the college gate. We were still waiting for Malini. I had called her twice in the last fifteen minutes and she had told me she would be there in two minutes. She sounded drunk on the phone.

'Hi, Avantika,' Malini said, a silly drunk smile on her face. Unlike mine, her suitcase was small and light and she lobbed it into the boot of the taxi herself.

'Hi, Malini.'

'I wouldn't be crying if I were you,' Malini said.

'Why so?' Avantika asked.

'He is doing this for you. You are one lucky girl, Avantika,' she said and smiled at Avantika.

'Isn't he sweet?' Avantika winked a knowing smile at Malini who looked away and slipped into the back seat with me. We waved and after the driver confirmed the destination, we were off. Avantika did not want to come to the airport for she did not want to see me go.

'I like your girl,' said Malini, putting on her huge bumblebee-type sunglasses to hide her reddened eyes.

'And she likes you, I guess.' I smiled. 'There is something so similar between the two of you.'

'So will you fall for me now?' she joked.

'Will you?'

'I have a boyfriend. If I didn't, then maybe,' said Malini and added, 'Avantika is too good for you.'

It wasn't the first time someone had pointed this out so I just nodded.

'So, how did you two land up together?'

'It is a long story,' I said. We got in the line, took our boarding passes and went through the security check. My mind raced back to how Avantika and I had started. We boarded the flight and Malini started that conversation again.

'We have a two-hour flight. I think now you can tell me your long story,' she said.

'I get airsick,' I said.

'That's why you should always be piss drunk before a flight.'

18

People clamoured to get their luggage out from the overhead bins like it was a race. Malini and I sat tight in our seat till the aircraft cleared and joined the ones who had won the race to the shuttle bus that took us to the airport building.

'That's an interesting story!' she said as we entered the Mumbai airport.

'I told you it was,' I said.

'So are they going to send us a car or what?' she asked as we picked up our bags from the conveyor belt.

'Malini, we are participants, not the chief guests!' I mocked.

'So do you know how to get there?'

'There must be taxis outside I believe.'

It turned out that there were plenty and they fought between themselves to catch our attention. We chose a taxi driver who looked like he wouldn't rip us off, and it took us an hour and a half to reach the college. Drenched in sweat, we were cursing the city and our decision to participate.

'I am already regretting coming here, Deb. You are an asshole,' said Malini.

I called up the festival coordinator and he came running to the main gate to receive us. His urgency in signing us in and making sure we got a comfortable room in the college's guest house calmed our nerves.

'I hope you don't snore,' she said.

'I don't,' I said. 'I hope you don't fart.'

'I do sometimes and people die when I do.' She frowned. 'At what time does the competition begin tomorrow?'

'It is at ten, I guess.'

'You want to go through the presentation again?'

'Sure. Shashank has made some changes and I guess they are good.'

'Nice,' she said and flipped open the laptop.

It was already ten in the night when we finished going through the presentation, making last-minute changes, altering the backgrounds and fonts a little so that the judges spent more time looking at the slides than trying to understand them. We divided our parts and we thought we were ready to go. I was unpacking when Malini's phone rang and she went outside the room to get it. She came back to the room, smiling, and I wondered if it was her boyfriend from back home.

'Guess what!' she said.

'What?'

'A friend called and she invited me to a party! She saw my status message on Facebook and knew that I was in Mumbai. It's going to be sweet.'

'So?' I asked.

'So? Let's go!' she said, excitedly as she rummaged through her luggage.

'I don't know your friend and we have the presentation tomorrow,' I pointed out.

'Don't be such a spoilsport. Let's go!' she said. She was already putting dresses on herself to decide which looked better. I was glad she didn't ask me because I would have been of no help at all. My protests against the idea were shot down and fifteen minutes later, we were on the Mumbai streets making our way to Trilogy—a newly opened hip lounge bar in Bandra—where supposedly all the rich kids and starlets hung out.

'So how do we get into this place?' I asked.

She looked at me like I had insulted who she was and I half expected her to say, 'Do you even know who I am?'

During our drive to the club, Malini's phone rang many times, and every time she was more excited about the whole affair. On our way we stopped at a wine and beer shop and she bought a quarter bottle of Smirnoff vodka, green apple flavour, and drank it all by herself. It smelled terrible and I thought I would never drink an apple-flavoured drink again.

'So? Who all are coming?' I asked.

'A whole bunch of people!' she said, a drunk, goofy smile pasted on her face. *Awkward.*

The club was lit in bright red and blue neon lights. The bouncers checked our names in the guest list and let us through, even bowed down and smiled. On the table facing the door, about fifteen people waved at Malini—girls, guys and obviously gay guys. Malini ran to them and hugged them one after the other, laughed and held hands—quite in contrast to how she used to behave in the college—as I walked slowly up to them and hoped the hugging business would end soon. The girls had come in the shortest of dresses possible. There were off-shoulders, dresses held up by the tiniest of fibres tied dangerously around their necks and sinfully short skirts. Wanting to be a good boy, I tried to concentrate on their faces, but could hardly look beyond the abundant tanned and untanned skin on display. They seemed to have stepped out of fashion catalogues. It felt awkward between all the unknown people but I did not mind the sight.

'This is Deb,' Malini announced.

Everybody shouted a big 'Hi', and I greeted them back. They were drunk. After the brief customary greetings were exchanged, none of which were audible in the din of the reverberating music, they turned towards the tequila shots lined up on the table. Tequila, the word itself reeks of hangover, but they weren't listening and started forcing it down my throat. I did not resist for I wanted the social awkwardness to end as soon as possible and being drunk seemed like a legit plan.

First shot.

It hit the head and burnt my throat. The music became louder and the lights felt harsh on my eyes.

Second shot.

It hit harder and my stomach burnt with an unseen ferocity, and slowly, the music blurred.

Third shot. Fourth shot. Fifth shot.

I lost count. It hit everywhere. My stomach calmed and my throat was soothed. The music ran through my body now and the lights seemed to converge into one big blob of different colours. Suddenly, everybody was a long-lost friend, a bhai, or a friend that I cursed for not having met before.

I picked up a bottle of beer and gave it a huge glug and emptied it in my belly like I had been thirsty for days. I do not remember the last time I drank so irresponsibly. It really did not matter what I was drinking, and everything tasted the same: a muted bitterness.

I felt someone tugging at my arm, and felt the blue and red rays of light pierce my eyes, enter the brain, and play lacrosse with it. My legs moved and so did my hands. I felt arms around me. I felt mine around someone else. Time slowed down. The faces blurred. Everyone looked the same. They all looked seductively beautiful and everyone danced well. The lights dimmed further and I felt bodies writhing against me. Was it Malini? Was it her friend in the green dress? I did not know. I still cannot tell.

Somewhere in all the sweat and writhing of bodies against me, the night ended for me. I faintly remember someone helping me into the taxi and asking me if I would be okay.

19

'Wake up. WAKE UP. WAKE UP.'
I heard these sounds ring in my head. Then I felt my shoulder shaking, then the whole of me and the bed with it. The bed was wet and I wondered for a moment if I had wet my bed. I was back to when I was seven years old and a bed-wetting young boy.

'Huh?' I opened my eyes to see Malini staring at me. Her voice hurt my ears. *I have not peed, it's my sweat.* 'What happened?'

'It's fucking ten!' screamed Malini.

'Huh? Ten?' I said, the significance still not registering in my head, and then it did. CASE STUDY! 'Oh . . . fuck, fuck, fuck.'

I stood up, my head hammered by a million sledgehammers, my tongue coated and my breath a weapon of mass destruction. I was terribly hung-over. Goddamn tequila. The room was in a mess and so was I.

'When did you wake up?' I asked her.

'Just now.' She was throwing her clothes all over the room trying to look for her formal suit and found it.

'Let's just get ready and rush,' I said.

'What do you think I am doing?' barked Malini.

I opened my suitcase and looked for my suit. We looked at each other and realized we did not have enough time to go out and change, so we turned our backs to each other and dressed up. As we changed in that room, I got a glimpse of her in the mirror on the wall, but it was unintentional. I did not mean to stare at her bare back but I wasn't sorry that I did.

We rushed through the hostel corridors while my head still pounded, and my hair was a dowdy mess and I could hardly walk straight. We entered the auditorium and waved at the co-coordinator. He was pissed off for he had been trying to reach us since morning.

'Where have you guys been? Now, we have scheduled you last in line,' he said, barely suppressing his displeasure.

We stared at the floor, hoping it would consume us. While the other teams gave their presentations, we brushed ourselves up and tried to look as presentable as we could. Quite obviously, she did a better job for she had the entire cosmetic industry hidden in the zips and crevices of her handbag.

'I hope you have the pen drive,' she asked.

'Yes, I do,' I said and we wished the best of luck to ourselves.

We were up next and I was a pile of nerves. I would not say we did our best, but we did the best we could with a hangover and thoughts of the day before running through our heads.

The result was out within fifteen minutes of our presentation. We did not feature in the list of winners. Not even a consolation prize. We lost. I lost.

~

'Hey! What happened? How did it go?' Avantika asked.

'We lost.'

'Oh . . . never mind. At least you tried,' consoled Avantika.

'But it went well?' she asked.

'Under the circumstances, yes,' I said.

'Under what circumstances?'

'We got a little drunk last night and woke up with a bad hangover this morning,' I explained and Malini punched me and gave me a nasty stare. 'What was that for?' she mouthed in whispers.

'You went drinking with her? Again?'

'It was a party and I couldn't say no. They just forced me to drink and I was—'

'A night before the presentation? How irresponsible can you get?' scolded Avantika.

'I am sorry. I didn't think I would drink that much.'

'Anyway, did you have fun though?'

'I guess. I do not remember most of it. I was out within the first three shots and the rest of the night is just a blur.'

She chuckled. 'At least you did something well!'

'I guess.'

'Come back soon now. I have had enough of you not being around,' she said.

'Yes, I will. I can't wait to see you again. Why does it feel like a month has passed and I haven't seen you? Feels like forever.'

'So what are your plans for tonight?' she asked. I saw Malini get restless by the long phone call.

'We might go out again.'

'Have fun! But don't do anything silly . . .'

'Silly?'

'Nothing, just come back soon, Deb,' she said.

'I love you, baby,' I muttered and Malini rolled her eyes.

'I love you,' said Avantika and disconnected the phone.

'You call her baby?' Malini mocked.

'So? Everyone uses it. What do you call your boyfriend?'

'I call him by his name. That's what names are for, you idiot,' she said.

'Whatever. If your boyfriend was lovable enough, you would have called him *baby* or anything else.'

She frowned. 'Why don't you start calling Avantika *jaan* or *jaanu*?'

'This conversation is over,' I grumbled.

She let the topic rest and we headed to the nearest bar to celebrate our effort, even though I wanted to go to McDonald's or someplace where they didn't serve drinks. Caravan was a decently done up place for its price and I liked it from the moment I stepped in even though the proximity of the bar and the bottles of alcohol made me want to throw up. We ordered the biggest pizza they had. She ordered a beer and I stuck with lime juice.

'Why did you hit me when I was on the phone?'

'I wanted you to shut up,' she said.

'Why?'

'You don't have to tell her everything!'

'What did I tell her?'

'Duh! That you went out with me last night and that you got sloshed. Girlfriends don't need to know every last detail of what you did or didn't do.'

'But I tell her everything. She doesn't mind and she doesn't have a problem. That's how it's always been,' I said. 'There is no reason to hide anything from her. Why should I feel guilty when there's no reason to feel so?'

I have always thought of Avantika as a witness to my life. She was someone who would see it all, someone who would know everything about me, someone who would always be there. And if my story ever needed to be told, she would be the one to tell it.

'Obviously she minds, everyone does. She just does a better job of hiding it.'

'She knows that I wouldn't do anything unwarranted,' I said confidently.

'Then you're lucky she doesn't know what happened last night.' She rolled her eyes again, and I wanted to tell her that her devil-may-care attitude was not going down well with me.

'Why is that smirk on your face?'

'Nothing.' She smiled.

'What happened last night?' I asked again.

'You really want to know?'

'Yes, please tell me.'

She kept nibbling at the crust of the pizza, ignoring my questioning eyes. I strained myself to piece together last night but everything that happened between the fourth shot and this morning never found a place in my head.

'You don't want to know. Even if you do, you would not be able to keep it to yourself. And I wouldn't want to get you in trouble with Avantika.'

'Shut up, Malini. Just tell me.'

'If you insist.' She smiled. 'Last night—' she paused.

'Go ahead.'

'Nothing happened.' She laughed and almost choked herself.

'Fuck you.'

She kept laughing and then suddenly stopped and said very seriously, 'Last night, you kissed three girls and none of them were Avantika.'

What! 'You are kidding, right?'

'No, Deb, I'm as serious as death,' she said. 'Look.'

Oh, no. She fished out her digital camera from her handbag and scrolled through the photographs from last night. In the initial photographs, everybody looked sane and we were just smiling in those pictures, and in most of them I was in the background with a beer bottle in hand, smiling goofily. No signs of kisses. As the night went on and we came to the later pictures, the hugs and the kisses became more intimate and scandalous. *This isn't true; this is some fucked-up Photoshop.*

I counted the number of times I was doing something I shouldn't have been doing; there were two unmistakable instances where my tongue was woefully digging inside another girl's mouth.

My mind went into multiple convulsions as I thought about the consequences. I did not even remember what any of the girls looked like. Or who they were! My heart sank to my feet and I slumped in my chair. It was right in front of my eyes yet I could not recall anything.

She would understand I was not in my senses. I do not even remember what happened last night. She would not accuse me. She would not leave me. What if she does? What if she doesn't believe me? What if she thinks I am lying? What if she did the same? Would I forgive her? Would I?

I felt like shit. Why did I do it!

'Fuck. Give me the camera.'

I deleted the pictures.

'Is that going to help?' asked Malini.

'Will you please stop smiling? This isn't funny. And *who* are these girls? Are they CRAZY? Why did they kiss me? *Sluts*.'

'Oye. Who are you calling sluts? What do you think you are, Deb? You kissed them back,' argued Malini.

'Sorry.' My breaths were short and ragged. 'Who was clicking these pictures?'

'I was,' said Malini and added as a matter of fact, 'and you also kissed me but there are no pictures for that.'

'This can't be true. You're shitting me, right? I couldn't have kissed you, could I?' I said and held my head when I saw her nodding. She was serious. 'I am so screwed.'

'Listen, Deb, no one remembers anything. These photographs mean nothing. Nobody has them and you just deleted them. No one has to know what happened last night.'

'But—'

'So you don't have to tell her. It was just a silly night and nobody will ever talk about it. It is as if it never happened. The pizza is getting cold. You need to eat.'

'But I know it did . . .'

I had already decided I would not tell her. I couldn't have. She had trusted me and there was no way I was breaking that.

~

On our way back to the room, Malini kept assuring me it was not a big deal and I should not feel guilty about it. 'You wouldn't even know what happened had I not told you,' she said, and even though it was wrong on so many levels I decided to believe her.

'Were you in your senses?' I asked her.

'As in?'

'I mean . . . did you know what was happening?'

'You mean if I knew I was kissing you?' she said as she lit her cigarette. She offered me one and I refused.

'So?'

'I did. Why are you obsessing so much about it, Deb? Nobody remembers. Nobody cares. It was a stupid night and that's how everyone will remember it.'

'I do. I care.'

'Stop being such a girl about it. I have an idea. Why don't we get sloshed again and think about it deeply? What say?' asked Malini and dangled the bottle of vodka in front of me.

'I don't think so. I'm still hung-over from last night.'

'Oh c'mon, Deb. And don't worry, I won't kiss you again. You are not my type,' said Malini and poured the drinks.

'Aren't we drinking too much?' I asked.

'I have to forget what happened too,' she said.

'You are not going to tell him?'

'No and neither should you,' she said. 'And there is no such thing as too much drinking! There's only too much thinking.'

20

As I walked out of the airport and my eyes scanned the crowd for her, my heart was heavy with the guilt it carried. I badly wanted to see her, and then I did.

'I missed you,' Avantika said as she hugged me.

'I missed you too.'

'You two make me cry,' Malini mocked. Avantika smiled at her.

'Hey, man,' Mittal said. 'Welcome back! Hi, Malini!' He smiled at her flirtatiously.

'Hi, Ganesh!' She smiled back.

'It's Mittal,' he corrected.

Avantika rolled her eyes. We drove back to college and I kept asking myself whether I should tell her. She was smiling excitedly, asking me about the presentation and our competition, and I did not want to snatch that away from her. *Stay shut*, I told myself. 'Relax, you look like shit,' Malini told me.

~

Things were worse by the afternoon.

Avantika wouldn't leave my side and wouldn't stop doting on me and telling me that she had missed me and every such

gesture made me feel worse about myself. I excused myself
and told Avantika I had to meet Shashank. She told me she
would miss me and I wanted to smash my head against a wall
and die. Malini's words kept ringing in my head.

I was being a girl. I really didn't need to tell Avantika
anything. She did not need to know something that I did not
even remember happened. I was not guilty of anything.

Shashank listened patiently, nodding his head, shaking
his head, while I narrated the incident to him, making sure
I didn't miss out any of the details. Farah was in his room as
well, nodding and judging me all the time, looking at me like
I was a diseased puppy and needed to be put down.

'Mittal would have been so proud of you,' said Shashank.

'I haven't told him. And you don't have to tell him,' I said.

'I will not. But I think you should tell Avantika. You might
fight for a few days, but things would be fine.'

'I don't want her to feel bad. I mean I don't even remember
what happened!' I tried to defend myself.

'All these arguments are okay, but you still need to tell
Avantika. If you tell her right now, she will know you love
her and you wanted to tell her. The later you tell her, the more
problems it will create.'

Farah nodded.

'If you want, I can talk to her,' Shashank said.

'Thank you, but I think I will do it,' I said.

'Anyway, you really don't remember any of the girls you
kissed?' Shashank asked and I shook my head.

I left his room and trudged to Avantika's room, trying to
rearrange my words. I knocked and she opened the door.

'We need to talk.'

'You?' she said. 'I thought you were with Shashank and Farah.'

I looked at her and she looked as beautiful as she always did.
She had just got up. Long, flowing hair covered a part of her

face and her eyes looked at me from behind those strands of hair—full of love, hope, optimism and belief. My eyes welled up wondering if that would be the last time we would meet like this, without an iota of distrust.

'I need to tell you something,' I said. 'Please don't be mad.'

She took me by my hand and made me sit down.

'I won't be,' she said.

I started from the point when Malini and I had reached the guest house in Mumbai. I narrated in detail everything that happened over the next two days. Her eyes began to quiver and her grip around my hand became loose and my hands began to tremble. Tears trickled down her cheeks and the light in her eyes slowly died out.

I cursed my existence. I cursed that moment of envy that had made me go to Mumbai; every tear of hers pained me and made my life a little bit more miserable. By the time I finished, she sat there, chipping at her nail polish as she sobbed softly.

'I am sorry. I don't deserve you, I guess,' I said.

I waited for her to say something. She just kept looking down at her hands. I felt terrible and decided that I should leave her alone. I stood up to leave when she reached out and held my hand.

'Avantika, I am really sorry—'

She did not let me complete my sentence. She stood up and hugged me as if she would never leave. I do not know how much time passed as we stood there hugging, crying; her body shivered in my arms.

'It's okay,' she muttered, as if to herself, justifying what I had done.

Avantika finally looked at me, held my face in her hands, and kissed me.

'Were those kisses better than this?' she asked.

'I told you I don't remember, and even if I did, it couldn't be.'

'You would compare?' she asked again.

'Never,' I said and hugged her.

I cried like a little girl bunched up at her knees and she patted my head to console me and told me it was all right and she had forgiven me. I promised never to do anything silly thereafter and she asked me not to feel sorry about it. Her goodness only made me feel guiltier about what I had done.

'So you did have a good time!' she mocked.

'Can you stop it now? I am feeling guilty enough already.'

'I am sorry.'

'I am sorry. Why are you sorry?'

'. . . because I am attaching so much importance to something you don't have any knowledge of doing.'

'You are way too sweet, Avantika.'

'I know that, you horny bastard. And what has happened to you? You are drinking too much. I asked you not to.'

'I am sorry. I will stop now. Sure.'

We kissed and made love, taking breaks to cry and to tell each other how much we were in love and that we would do nothing that would endanger our relationship.

It was love. It is usually very stupid for guys to put up status messages on Facebook telling the world how much they love their girls; that is usually reserved for the girls to do. But moments like these make you want to tell the world how much in love you are—put up a status message in capital letters. I contemplated putting it up, but the testosterone kicked in and I decided to be a man.

After all, I did not need the world to know. I only wanted her to know what she meant to me.

I kept whispering 'I love you' into her ears until she dozed off, hoping I could hypnotize her into believing that she needed me for the rest of her life.

21

Avantika cried for a few days, mostly in solitude, before she came to terms with it. She said she was being irrational and she said she understood how I must not have known what I was doing. Avantika had been a raging alcoholic and a drug addict during her early college days. She knew what it was like to get hammered and carried away.

I had just finished eating when Malini waved at me from a distance; Mittal was sitting next to her with a bowl full of watery daal and a roasted poppadom. I had not talked to her for the last few days. I had just texted her to tell her that I had told Avantika everything about us and things were fine.

'Hey,' Mittal called me over.

'Hi,' I acknowledged her presence with a smile.

'Hi, Deb,' she said.

'Not coming for the class?' I asked them.

'Mittal is taking me out for a movie,' said Malini and Mittal smiled at me—a wicked, *eat-that* smile.

'Oh that's nice.'

'Why don't you come along too?' she asked and Mittal vigorously shook his head to ask me to turn down the offer.

'Thank you, but short attendance, can't come. Maybe next time.'

'Fine,' she said.

I took their leave and heard them laughing as I walked away from them. Mittal was on to her in a flash. Not bad at all. I wondered if Malini had told him about what had happened in Mumbai.

'Mittal is cute. I wonder how he's still single,' Malini had told me in Mumbai. I thought she wasn't serious. The retail franchise class was boring. The professor kept making obvious flowcharts on the board expecting us to ask questions, and I couldn't stop thinking about what Mittal and Malini were doing. Maybe I should have accompanied them to the movie. Maybe next time.

~

'Where is Mittal? He is not picking up the phone. He has to report to the placement committee office at ten,' grumbled Shashank and tried to reach him again.

'I don't know. He went to watch a movie with Malini in the afternoon, haven't had a word since then.'

'Call Malini,' he said.

'Why? Is it important?'

'Obviously!' he said, pissed off.

Shashank had our passwords to our official MDI email IDs and handled everything that needed to be taken care of. That day, Mittal had received a mail from the placement committee and every mail from them was important and sacrosanct. The students on the placement committee were responsible for our placements and hence they wielded unquestionable power over other students. They were equally hated and respected.

I called up Malini, and Mittal picked up the call. I could hear Malini giggle in the background and I felt like she shouldn't.

'Hey.'

'Where the fuck are you?' I asked him.

'I am at a friend's flat,' he said.

'Flat? What are you doing there? Weren't you watching a movie?'

At this Shashank snatched the phone from me and blasted him for ignoring mails from the placement committee; he was furious.

While they accused each other of screwing up, I felt strange to think Malini was up to something with Mittal. I could not put a finger on why it felt a little quirky. I let the feeling pass. It took him an hour to reach the college and I was a little restless until they reached. I felt guilty that I actually cared about those two being together.

'When did I have to report?' he asked as he approached us. Malini followed closely behind.

Shashank asked Mittal not to act fresh with the placement committee guys. They were a bunch of arrogant, snotty people, and Shashank told Mittal what excuse he should give them. Mittal nodded and went inside the office. Shashank left to meet Farah soon after and asked me to take care of Mittal.

'How was the movie?'

'We didn't watch it,' Malini said.

'Aha,' I smirked. 'What did you do then?'

'Oh please. Nothing happened,' she blew me off.

'I never said anything happened.'

'But you meant that, Deb.'

'I didn't,' I said.

'Don't give me those jealous-boyfriend looks,' she said. 'Anyway, why have they called him?'

'No idea. And I gave you no looks, Malini!' She rolled her eyes. 'Seriously!' I asserted.

We waited for a couple of minutes before he came out of

the room with his head hung low and a dead expression on his face. Something had gone wrong.

'What's the matter?' Malini asked him. He looked at us with mournful eyes and sagging shoulders.

'I got PLACED! I FUCKING GOT A JOB! EAT THAT, MOTHERFUCKERS!' shouted Mittal and pointed in the direction of the academic building.

He threw his hands around me and picked me up. My bones were crushed in his grip and I could hardly fathom what happened to the girls he dated.

'This is incredible. I'm so happy for you,' I said and we shook hands like men.

We called up Shashank and Avantika and told them about the offer and they were excited for him. It was a big day for him, and for us.

'Where are you taking us tonight?' Avantika asked as she walked into the canteen a few minutes later.

'Today?'

'Why? What's the problem with today?' she asked.

'Shashank isn't here. He told me he had to go somewhere with Farah and he couldn't say no to her,' Mittal said. 'Such a pussy.'

'You can take him out some time else. Do not lose this moment!' she argued.

'Where do you want to go?'

We decided on a new unaffordable nightclub near MDI that we had never thought we would go to. Night-outs at Management Development Institute were far and few since we were expected to turn up at sharp 8.30 a.m. every day for an early morning dosage of accounting or international marketing.

'You need to join us,' Mittal told Malini who was quiet all this while.

'Thank you, but I can't. I have some work to do,' said Malini.

'Like what? Getting drunk alone?' Mittal retorted. 'You're coming with us or I'm not celebrating today.'

Malini frowned. 'Okay. Fine. You're such a brat.'

'Yay! Thank you,' Mittal said.

While Mittal and Malini argued on whether he was a brat or not, I could see Avantika shifting in her place. She did not look too comfortable with Malini tagging along but she could not have said anything.

22

'It is fucking ten thirty, man,' Mittal said, pacing in the mess, angry, his gelled hair now falling out of place.

'Girls.'

'Call Avantika. Malini isn't picking up.'

I called up Avantika and she did not pick up either. The last time she had picked up, she had said she would be ready in five minutes and it had been half an hour since then. It wasn't until another twenty minutes had passed that they showed up.

And I am not kidding when I say that every eyeball in the college cafeteria turned towards them as they sashayed towards us in their short dresses, radiant faces and beautifully done-up hair.

Avantika wore a flaming-red off-shoulder dress that ended a few inches above her knees. Her bright red stilettos made her look almost as tall as me. She had left her hair open and she flashed a big enrapturing smile as her eyes met mine. Her eyes had never looked as big and captivating as they looked then. She had never looked more beautiful. I do not know how many times I had said this to her in the last three years.

'Stop staring. Let's go.' She winked.

'You just kill me every time.'

'I know. That's the intention.' She smiled.

97

She was a work of art. It was only later that I noticed that Malini chose a little black dress that evening, and yes, I have to admit, she looked raging hot.

Avantika, the quintessential beauty, versus Malini, the hot temptress—it was a fair match and neither Mittal nor I were complaining.

'Let's go?' Mittal said as he put the car in gear.

'I love what you are wearing,' Malini said.

'Thank you. You look pretty! If only I were not straight,' Avantika answered. They both laughed out and hugged. To see two extremely hot women touch each other is such an undeniably remarkable sight. No wonder good old girl-on-girl action porn always finds space in every guys' hidden folders.

'I am sure MDI has never seen such beautiful things before,' Mittal said to me.

The 'things' comment didn't go down too well with the girls in the back seat whose feminist genes kicked in and they bashed us for being dishonourable, chauvinistic pigs. We were not to blame though, not as much. They looked hot—as if they had come straight out of magazines that guys take to their washrooms for a little *alone time*.

Mittal kept the mood chirpy, regaling us with anecdotes from his illustrious school and undergraduate college days, until we reached there, while I was just busy looking at Avantika and sometimes at Malini. They were innocent glances, that's all they were. It took us just over an hour to get there.

'It's very flattering, but will you stop staring?' said Avantika and walked ahead of me.

Malini nudged me from behind. 'She does look awesome, doesn't she?'

I nodded and added, 'So do you.' She smiled.

We entered the gates and immediately knew why this place was so highly rated; the huge dance floor was lit up with a maze of laser lights of a million different colours. The place stunk of money, brats and expensive alcohol. It felt that we were late because drunken couples were making out everywhere, and I tried not to think of that night in Mumbai.

'Here we are!' Mittal shouted out to our deaf ears.

'Let's get drunk!' Malini joined in. Avantika shouted out her approval.

'What will you guys have?' Malini asked all of us as she pushed and shoved her way to the counter.

She ordered shots for all of us. Avantika was the designated driver for the night so she refused to have any.

'Can we dance? Or you need to be more drunk?' Avantika asked me, a little miffed at my decision to drink that day. I could already see her feet moving even while she was sitting. She was a great dancer; the Bharatanatyam and Odissi lessons she had taken as a child gave her an innate sense of rhythm and music and made her aware of her body and what it could do.

'Just one more,' I shouted back. 'Or maybe two!'

One more went on until I was seven shots down. Or was it eight? I had started to grope or feel her up but she pulled me on to the dance floor, slapping my hands away from her body. We fought our way to the middle of the dance floor, which was now crowded with drunk girls and drunk men flailing their arms around like they knew how to dance.

Avantika held me by the neck and pulled me into her as we grappled for space on the floor. 'Dance,' she whispered in my ear as if I knew how to, and then held my hands and placed them on her waist and writhed in my grasp. Her eyes never left mine, and she turned and twisted and gyrated against my body. I just stared, a little turned on, a little surprised and drunk out of my senses. And then almost like nobody was watching us, she turned and pulled me close, and her tongue unapologetically wandered in my mouth. Just when I grabbed her to kiss her back, she pushed me back and led me off the dance floor.

'What happened?' I asked her, my tongue flapping like a fish out of water.

'Let's keep something for the night, shall we?'

'As you say.'

She excused herself for a little girl time and left for the washroom as I glugged down the rest of my drink that I had left on the table. It had become warm, but it had no taste, not to me. I looked at my watch. It had been more than an hour that we had been dancing and it hardly felt like it. I ordered another drink and looked around for the other two. I ran my eyes over scores of little black dresses but I could not find hers. I wondered if Mittal and Malini had something going by then and it made me squirm.

But then I found Malini sitting in a corner, drinking a red cocktail from a long twirling straw. She sat alone, cross-legged, her perfectly sculpted legs shining under the club's lights. The jogs around the campus really showed their effect as she had never looked hotter. I went up to her, flopped on the couch next to her and suppressed an urge to run my fingers over her naked thighs. *YOU'RE DRUNK*, I reprimanded myself.

'Where is he?'

'He?' she asked. Her eyes were rolling up. She was definitely drunk. 'Oh, he has just gone for a smoke.'

'You didn't go, you Toronto-returned babe?' I mocked. I was drunk, yet I knew that I wasn't being funny and wanted to drown in her cocktail. I just wanted to shut up and stop looking.

'No, I am just a little too drunk to smoke right now,' she said and put both her arms around my neck.

'Yes. You seem so,' I said, my head still spinning.

'And you are so sweet,' she said, her eyes losing focus, and closing.

'Thank you.'

She leaned further into me.

'You are such a nice guy,' she said, then touched my nose with her finger and tapped it.

'You are not all that bad either.'

I felt her pushing her body against mine, closer and closer still; her hands held my face and pulled it closer to hers till it hovered centimetres away and her breath warmed up mine as it wafted from her parted lips to mine. I felt her lips brush against mine. Her perfume overwhelmed my nostrils and she looked deep into my eyes with those limpid wet eyes of hers and asked me to come closer. Her lips enveloped mine. And mine hers; I felt the wetness on my lips.

'Deb?' I heard, amidst all the noise. I looked up and found Avantika staring directly at me, and she didn't look pleased at all.

23

We had not spoken for an hour. She stood by the door and I sat on the bed. I could hear the silent sobs. She did not look at me once in all this while and it was killing me from inside. I did not know what to say; I didn't deserve to say anything to her. Sitting there rewinding repeatedly in my mind what had happened, I cursed myself. I wondered if that was the last time I would be in her room. I wondered if that was the end of *us*. I was praying she would say something and not stand there and cry. It was becoming unbearable and I just wanted to hug her and say that I was sorry. But sorry? Again? I didn't deserve to use that word again.

I had kissed the same girl, twice in fifteen days. This time I was not even drunk and I knew exactly what was happening there in the club. I was *not* drunk. There was no excuse this time.

I needed to look into myself this time before talking to Avantika. *What did I just do? Why did I kiss Malini? Was it a mistake? Twice?*

'Deb,' she said, her voice as cold as steel. The gravity in her voice shook me and it was a harbinger of tough times, I could tell.

'Yes.' My voice trembled.

'You should go now.'

'What?' I said. *I should go? Like forever? Is that what she means?* I hoped not and I did not move. I did not want to. *What have I done?*

'You should leave,' she said. 'Just go.'

'But—' I said, yet I had nothing to say.

'Please don't say anything, just go, Deb.'

I left the room, my eyes stuck at her until she closed the door. I saw those eyes, stricken and filled with tears and thought maybe it was best to leave her alone. I walked through the corridors, my head hung low and tears streaked down my cheeks.

'Just go, Deb.'

I felt sick in the pit of my stomach and I felt I would be sick, like physically sick. I went to my room and logged into Gmail. She pinged me as soon as I was online.

Avantika: Why, Deb? Why?

Me: I am sorry, Avantika. I don't know how it happened. I am really sorry. I love you. You know I do. Don't you? ☹

Avantika: Whatever I saw today makes me doubt everything, Deb. You shared a room with her for two nights. God knows what happened then? What are you not telling me?

Me: For the sake of everything we have shared over the last few years, please believe me. I am not lying. I will never lie to you. She just came on to me.

Avantika: Don't give me that. I saw you. Don't just put it on her.

Me: I am sorry, Avantika. I know it is hard to trust me, but please, baby, I love you, and I love you more than anything in this world. Please, you know that.

Avantika: But it is not good enough. How do I forget what I saw? I was right there, Deb, right there! Would you have accepted it?

Me: I am sorry.

Avantika: I want to forgive you. I really do. But I really don't know what to do.

Me: Avantika, don't do this.

Avantika: I just think we should stay away for a little time.

Me: Please don't? I wouldn't be able to take it. Please, don't do this to me.

Avantika: Let me figure out things. Give me some time. Let's take a break. Till that time just think whether you would forgive me for the same.

Me: I would.

Avantika: No, you wouldn't.

Me: Are you leaving me?

I had tears in my eyes as I wrote this.

Avantika: I never said that. I just want to be alone for a little while. And probably you need to get a few things straight too. Take this time to do it.

Me: Baby, don't do this. Please, let me come to you. I am sorry. Please.

Avantika: Deb, please. All I am asking from you, please, don't contact me for a few days. Please. I love you, Deb. I always will, but please?

Me: How long, baby?

Avantika: I will tell you. Bye, baby. Take care.

I was crying now. I was frantic, shaking. *She cannot do this to me*, I thought. But she could. She had just done it.

Me: Bye.

Avantika: Best of luck.

She went offline and I felt like my head would implode. I sent offliners but she did not reply. I sent a zillion mails asking for forgiveness, pouring my heart out, even threatening that I would end myself if she didn't reply. I wrote to her to tell her how much she meant to me and how much I hated myself for what I had done but she did not reply. I called her, but she cut the phone every time and texted me not to call her.

Her message read:

I love you, Deb. But I need some time alone. Please give me that. I trust you and whatever you feel for me. Just let me be with myself for a few days. Please don't message and call me to make it worse. Please. I beg you.

I was choking on my own tears, wailing like an old woman, howling. I felt angry and disgusted at myself and at Malini. I wanted to call up Shashank but I felt ashamed. *What would I say to him?* I re-read the chat a million times; my eyes never left my Google Talk contact list to see if she had unblocked me.

The room came on to bite me. I kept texting her about how much I wanted her back and how I would make things right, but she did not reply.

The worst part was that I did not even have an answer for myself. What I did was a stupid, horny mistake . . . but why? I knew it was wrong, but why did I do it? I wished I could undo the last twelve hours. I wished I had never known Malini.

Every time the phone beeped, my heart pounded only to be dampened for it would not be her. The calls went unanswered.

I waited for the morning class where I would get to see her again. Time came to a standstill; every minute seemed like an hour, laborious and torturous. *Things will be fine*, I told myself. I closed my eyes, and hoped that when I would wake up, it would all be gone. Like a bad dream. I consoled myself that she would read all the messages and feel for me.

The next morning, I woke up half an hour before time and didn't shave or brush my hair, for I thought it would invoke pity. I waited outside the class but she did not come. The professor entered the class and she was still nowhere to be seen. I wondered if she was okay. I took the seat where we usually used to sit. After five minutes, she entered the class;

one innocent smile with a believable excuse is all it took her to get attendance. She sat on the first seat.

I texted her but it looked like she had left the phone in her room. So I wrote a note to her on a piece of paper and asked the person sitting next to me to pass it along to her. She read it, crumpled it. She looked behind and her eyes seemed to say, *Please leave me alone.* There was no escaping it. The class crawled to its finish and Avantika left the class in a hurry. I walked behind her, but clearly, she did not want to talk to me. Or even look at me. I felt disgusted with myself for what I had done to her. She entered the girls' hostel and I stood there, hoping she would at least look back once and acknowledge my presence. She did not and I trudged back to the room. I sent her a few more texts hoping she would check her phone messages once she got back to her room.

I signed into Google Talk, with the only hope that she would have unblocked me. She surprisingly had. Never had I been more relieved or happy to see the tiny red dot against a name on that list. *Is the break over?*

Avantika: What if I had done the same with Kabir?

Me: Don't say that, baby.

Avantika: I am sorry. Give me some time, Deb. I will be fine. I miss you. Bye.

She signed off and blocked me again. I read the conversation repeatedly. The first sentence was as hurting as the last one was comforting. She missed me and I smiled. I closed my eyes and tried to catch up on some sleep between the two classes, forcing myself to dream of a time when Avantika and I would be together again.

24

'Still fighting?' Mittal asked.
'She is not talking to me.'

'It will be fine. Malini asked me to tell you that she is sorry,' he said and for the first time, Mittal sounded *sorry*.

Malini was not in the class. *Slut*, I said to myself.

Mittal told me Malini was not answering his calls and had asked him to *fuck off*. *Guilt*, I figured. I had got used to the feeling in the past few days. It kills you and empties you from the inside. The class ended and Avantika walked out of the class without even looking at me once. I felt deserted and lonely. It was a disease and it was affecting every part of me. Even Shashank had left with Farah on a small vacation to Lansdowne.

Back in the room, I spent hours lying prostrate on my bed, staring at the ceiling, wishing I were dead. My phone lay beside me and it hadn't rung in days. She was not calling every few minutes like she did. How I wished she had something to call me for: an assignment, maybe an extra class, something! Anything!

Everything in the room reminded me of her. I fiddled with my phone and called her a few times. But she didn't pick up, hardly denting my ego or self-pride; I would call her again in a bit. I left my room as it got hard for me to stay there any longer. Walking aimlessly around the campus, kicking stray stones didn't help either. I saw her everywhere, in couples that were sitting around, talking about the next quiz, the placement season and CGPAs, in the small cafes around the campus.

I walked past a bench on which we often spent our nights talking about the past that we had seen and the future that lay in front of us. A part of me hoped she would miss me and come to that bench too. A few joggers ran past me and between them, I saw Malini running.

Slut, I thought, just like I was.

25

It had been a week and every evening I had seen her jog past that bench. Sometimes, she had tears in her eyes but I never felt pity. If anything, I was still angry at her. Despite that there were times when I had thought of calling out her name and talking to her. I had not talked to anyone in over a week and I could do with some company.

I called out her name and she stopped. We stood there looking at each other for quite some time, not knowing what to say. I did not know what she was thinking but my mind battled with the thought of abusing her for screwing up everything.

'You wouldn't want to talk to me,' she cried aloud.

'I shouldn't,' I shouted back. She started walking away, still crying.

'Malini!' I shouted out again. 'Maybe I should.'

'Maybe you should not,' she wailed out. She stuck her earphones back in her ears and ran away; I stood there watching her go.

~

One day, she stopped running when she saw me sitting on the bench looking straight at her. I was waiting for her. Without a word she came and sat near me. An hour passed but we hadn't talked. She fiddled with her earphones. A tear or two trickled down her cheeks occasionally. I could not care less. I just sat there and tried to figure out just one answer . . . 'Why, Deb?' Why had I kissed her? It became clear to me that it was just the alcohol. I had no feelings for her whatsoever. Seeing her cry didn't move me.

'I am sorry,' she said, breaking the silence that hung like death between us.

'Hmm . . .'

'I really didn't mean to . . .'

'I know.'

'I am such a whore,' she said.

Maybe you are, and maybe I am, too. I had spent hours thinking about what made me do what I did, and it didn't make sense.

'I am sorry for ruining it,' she said.

'Nothing is ruined. She will come back. I will make her come back.'

'You can't do that if you sit next to me,' she said.

'Hmm . . .'

'I should go.'

'Maybe.'

She shook my hand, wished me luck and walked away. And suddenly in a moment, I had no one to talk to again.

26

The nights were even harder. The darker it got the more painful it became. I closed my diary, the repository of all the beautiful things I had shared with her: the big fights, the big loves, the big surprises, the birthdays and the anniversaries.

I had time, loads of it, and I didn't know what to do with it, so I sat and I thought about her till my head hurt. It felt like somebody was stabbing me repeatedly and those stabs never missed the heart. I became restless, and I wanted to walk up to her room and bang on her door and ask for forgiveness. But all she wanted was a few days alone. I took a deep breath and told myself that everything would be fine.

'It will be fine, man,' Shashank said, his voice cracking.

I could hear Farah in the background, shouting at him for something; their vacation was going as planned. I could have been with him, buried in a warm duvet with Avantika, laughing and kissing, our toes intertwining. I cut the line and apologized for disturbing him. My mind was now stuck there. Every trip that Avantika and I had gone on flashed in front of my eyes.

Kasauli. Rishikesh. Goa. Mumbai. The long talks on the balconies, the early morning bed teas, the late-night snuggles, the morning showers, the 'cancel-all-plans-and-stay-here' looks, the pecks, even the packing and the unpacking—it all came right in front of my eyes. I slept peacefully that day, without a worry, without a frown, with a lot of love in my heart, images of her in my eyes and the hope in my heart that things would be fine the next day.

~

The days were not getting any better. I obsessed about tracking every movement of hers; from her room to the class, from the library to the mess, from the mess to the classroom . . . I was losing my shit. My only consolation was to see her crying occasionally, and it gave me a glimmer of hope that she missed me and wanted me back as much as I wanted her. It had been two weeks now and there was nothing more comforting than watching her every day.

Once every few days, I would buckle down and bombard her with calls, messages and mails and all she did was to tell me sweetly that she needed time and she still loved me. I could never say anything beyond it.

Over the last few days, all the study groups had started working on their assignments, which meant Avantika was spending a lot of time with her group and Kabir. To see her with Kabir felt unimaginably painful, like someone slowly pulling all my hair, one by one. I put myself in her place and tried to imagine what it must have been like for her to see me with Malini that day in the club.

The few hours that I spent on the bench became a regular affair, a habit. I used to sit there and wait for Avantika to come. She never did but I saw Malini every day on her evening jog with a dead look on her face, earphones hanging loosely in front of her, and tears in her eyes. I could see her pick up pace as she approached the bench. We avoided eye contact.

Sometimes I thought of calling out her name, but then I would decide otherwise.

~

'Get over her!' Mittal told me.

'Mittal, it's just a break.'

'That is exactly what I am trying to tell you. She will come back. Just wait for her. Why do you have to follow her around!' he explained and lit a cigarette. He blew two smoke rings, the second one smaller than the first, and blew the second ring right through the first one. He smiled, impressed with himself.

'I am not following her around.'

'You are . . . if you had it your way you would have gone to the movie hall today and waited till the movie got over,' he said.

'Movie hall?' I asked.

'What? They have gone for a movie, right?'

'Who? They?'

'Kabir and Avantika.'

'What?' I said, as I spontaneously internally combusted.

Shashank, who had been quietly working on a case study all this time, now spoke up, 'Stop kidding, Mittal.'

They exchanged a nervous stare. Shashank knew too. They had gone for a movie and I was the last one to know. *Simply fucking great!* Mittal told me her whole study group had planned to watch a movie but people had dropped out, leaving just the two of them. Fuming, I left the room, despite the repeated pleas of Mittal and Shashank to relax. I went to my room and checked the newspaper for the places where the movie was playing. A quick permutation calculation told me that I had to be at ten places at the same time to be sure I could catch them after the movie; there was no way I could have guessed where they had gone.

I decided to wait.

My heart pounded as my eyes followed the second hand on my watch turn. I left my room and headed for the main gate of our college. I walked around in circles, sat, drank cups of coffee, answered roughly to the guards, who seemed concerned, and desperately tried to make time go faster. My eyes were stuck on the approach road to MDI and I looked for his car. I had been waiting for four hours for them to come back from that wretched movie.

I saw both of them sitting in the car, laughing, as it whizzed past me. The car did not enter the MDI gate, it just went straight ahead. *Where the fuck are they going now?*

~

It was eight in the night and she had switched off her phone after my twentieth call. The classes of the other sections were over and students had started idling in the open grounds of the campus; joggers were out jogging.

They had been together for seven hours now. Exhausted and angry, I walked around the campus, directionless and lost. As a last-ditch effort, I called on Kabir's number but a woman said in an irritating voice, 'The phone number you're trying to reach is out of coverage area.' I slumped down on the bench. I waited for Malini to run past me.

~

'What's the matter?' asked Malini.

'Nothing.'

I sighed and put my words in order. 'She is out with Kabir today.'

'I know. I saw them leave the campus,' said Malini and added after a pause, 'Don't think too much.'

'I wish.'

'You want to talk about it?' she asked me.

'Maybe not.'

'I am stinking right now, so let me just come back in five. And if you're still here by that time, we can talk,' said Malini.

'I don't want to talk about that bastard,' I said.

'Fine,' said Malini with a grin and walked away.

I held my head in my hands and waited for her to come back. I had once asked Avantika, when we had started going out, what she would think of the girl who would make me cheat on her. Avantika had said she would not blame the girl. 'Why shouldn't she have her share of fun?' she had asked. But I blamed Kabir. He knew everything about the two of us, and was still trying to charm his way into her life.

It was dark and most of the students had returned to the hostels to complete assignments, prepare presentations, and maybe, just to catch up on some sleep. Malini, smelling of fresh flowers and detergent, came and sat next to me.

'Did you ask her how the movie was?' asked Malini.

'That's not funny.'

'No, it isn't,' she said as she lit up a cigarette. 'Want one?'

'No, thank you.'

'Want to talk about what happened?' she asked.

'I don't know. She just wanted a break for a little while. It has been more than fifteen days now. Now, this Kabir issue, it is totally freaking me out and I don't know what to do.'

'It's just a phase. It will go away. You want me to talk to her?' she said.

'No, it is fine.'

'Please let me do something for you. The guilt is killing me. And it won't go until I see you both together,' she said and I saw those tears again in her eyes.

'We will be together,' I said. It was more of a wish than a belief.

'I hope so.'

'Anyway, how's your boyfriend? Samarth, was it? Did you tell him?'

'There is nothing to talk about him.' She looked away from me, closed her eyes and blew the smoke out from her nostrils. 'And I don't want to talk about him.'

I sat there wishing her life sucked more than mine. She took long drags on her cigarette which burnt to a bright orange. She said, 'He cheated on me.'

'Did you use me to get back at him?'

'Do you think I would need to use you? I could have used your friend,' grumbled Malini, 'Mittal. I kissed you because I was angry and drunk. That's all there is to it. It was a mistake. I'm sorry.'

'Don't be.'

'I am. I really didn't intend to use you.'

'I was just thinking you did it to me because you thought I was hot,' I joked; it wasn't even funny to me.

'You are irresistible,' she mocked and lit up another cigarette. While it hung limply from her lips, she muttered, 'Don't you see all the girls lining up?'

'Don't push it.'

'I have been told my sarcasm is endearing,' said Malini.

'It's not,' I corrected.

After a while she said, 'Avantika wouldn't like it if she knows that you were with me.'

'She is out with Kabir, isn't she?'

'Revenge won't help you win her back,' she said.

'It's not revenge. Shashank and Mittal are both sceptical about the way I am reacting to the whole situation, so I really can't talk to them. And I don't want to tell anyone else about it.'

'Why do you care if they know?' asked Malini, and as if to prove that she didn't, she waved at a couple that passed by us. 'I seriously don't give a fuck.'

We sat there for an hour, and we didn't talk; she smoked and I hoped there was nothing to worry about.

~

That night, as I ambled around the cafeteria, fiddling with my phone, avoiding eye contact with my classmates lest they saw my reddened eyes, I saw Avantika walking to the library, bundles of notes stuck precariously in her armpit, a pen clenched between her teeth. Our eyes met for a brief awkward moment. She hurried past me before I could say anything.

Back in the hostel, Kabir was sleeping, still in his shoes. Suppressing an urge to smother him with a pillow, I walked back to my room and opened the research methodology book with the hope of studying for the pop quiz next day, but the thought was ambitious. Almost involuntarily, I dialled her number and she cut the line immediately.

I texted her to ask where she had been the entire day, and she texted me back telling me she was busy and she didn't have the time to read my texts. Kabir's ugly face flashed in front of my face, and he was laughing, cursing and telling me that I had lost Avantika, and that he would be the one taking her out on dates and movies and romantic sojourns. Angry and frustrated, I called Malini.

'Hey,' she said.

'What are you doing?' I asked her.

'You seem to be angry.'

'That is because I am,' I said. 'Can I see you at the canteen?'

A few minutes later, Malini and I were walking towards the canteen nearest to the library. She was carrying a book on retail finance in her hands, the pages of which were folded and colour coded.

'Do you need to study?' I asked.

She laughed. 'No, not really. I'm hoping to pass the exams by my undeniable charm. Where's Avantika? Did you get to talk to her?'

'Library,' I said.

'Slow down,' she said as she tried hard to keep pace with me as I walked towards the canteen. She touched my shoulder in order to tell me to take it easy; it was awkward and she withdrew her hand.

At the canteen, we ordered noodles and pulled up chairs under the solitary street light. The noodles were hot, watery and spicy, just as I liked them.

'So how long do we plan to sit here and look at the library? I could have got my stalker binoculars,' she said. Then added wistfully, 'You are so hopelessly in love with her, aren't you?'

'I am just okay*ishly* in love,' I said, trying not to sound sissy. 'I am sorry to have got you here.'

'I am the very reason you are here. You needn't be sorry. I needed to get out of the room anyway,' she said.

I ate my noodles in silence and she flipped through her book, making small notes in the margins as she went. When distracted, she would tell me about her life back in Toronto— about her school, about the beautiful freckled white boys she dated as a schoolgirl. I listened to her intently as I finished her noodles as well, which she said were too spicy for her taste. Time and again, she would ask me about my old days in school, and I would tell her about my weight problem, and how I was teased for being fat and unhandsome for the greater part of my school life. 'Thank God you look dapper now!' she said. 'No, I don't,' I said.

There was no sign of Avantika.

'Let's go,' I said.

'Where? Library?' she asked.

'No. Back to the hostel. I have wasted enough of your time. You really need to mark the hell out of your book and use some more highlighters.'

'As you say,' she said.

As I walked past the library, I saw Avantika, her head buried in a thick book, and she looked rather fine. Right across the table, Kabir sat with the same book, underlining furiously.

'He's there, too,' I grumbled. 'He was in his room an hour back. I saw him.'

'You should have killed him when you had the chance,' responded Malini with a straight face.

I tried not to smile. 'I should have.'

27

Kabir and Avantika had started to spend a lot of time together. They had become like a word from a dictionary which when newly learnt mysteriously pops up in every article that you read. Wanting to get back at her, I started to spend a lot of time with Malini, hoping she would notice, feel jealous and helpless and come crying to me. I would, then, heroically sacrifice my bond of friendship with Malini to keep her happy; and in exchange would ask for nothing but for her to banish Kabir from her life. But she couldn't care less.

Has she moved on? I found myself asking the question.

I often argued with myself that I should not be around Malini, but every time I saw Avantika with Kabir, I just had to call Malini up. If it was hard for her, it was hard for me too. I needed someone too. Malini was my only way out of depression. That day, we had planned to watch a movie together since Shashank had told me that he had seen Kabir and Avantika hanging out together at a mall where he had gone with Farah.

It was hot and by the time we reached the movie hall in my old Maruti Zen, which had seen much better days in the past decade, we were sweating and I was embarrassed.

'Should have taken my car,' pointed out Malini.

'I guess,' I said; my shirt was wet and stuck to my skin. I stood in the line to buy our tickets, flapping my hands and jerking my head like a drenched dog.

'What is love to you?' asked Malini.

'I don't know,' I said irritably.

'Don't be so lame,' she said as we stood in line for popcorn.

'I can't put it in words,' I said. 'My shirt's still so wet. Should I go stand under the dryer in the washroom? That should do it.'

'We are in a management course. This is what we should be good at.' She smiled.

'Fine. Let me try.'

'Please do,' she said.

'Love isn't a feeling for me, it's her. She is pretty much my definition for it. I mean she taught me what it was. She made me feel what it was. She made me do all the insane things that I did for her, things that we did together, things that she did for me. Over the last three years, she has been love for me. She still is . . . always will be. I had once heard in a movie that the power in a relationship lies with the one who cares less. Before Avantika came around, I had always been powerful because I cared less and always protected myself from getting hurt. Avantika changed that. She changed me . . .' I paused. 'We should go in . . .'

The movie started and people rushed in.

'We should stay. It's cold inside and with your wet shirt, you will catch a cold. Anyway, this is better,' she took my hand and pulled me to the food court. She ordered lattes for both of us, and I ordered french fries with extra ketchup. 'Continue.'

'Continue?'

'Whatever you were saying about love . . . and her,' said Malini. 'Interesting stuff.'

'I said what I had to. I just love her. I don't know what love is, or how it is supposed to be, but she is the closest I will ever get to it.'

'She changed you, you said. So what were you? A player . . . because you don't look like one.' She laughed.

'Whatever.'

'Aww! But you do look cute, when you get all lovey-dovey and stuff. No wonder she adores you. You're like a little lost puppy.'

'Thank you, but nowadays, she adores that son of a bitch.'

'C'mon. Don't be such a kid. She will come back. Kabir is not her kind of guy.'

'I know. Somehow I fear she will not. I cheated on her and now, I am sitting with the same girl I cheated on her with, while she is on a break. And I didn't say that to make you feel guilty again.'

She shrugged. 'Samarth got drunk and made out twice with two different girls in three days. It is acceptable, as long as the girlfriend doesn't get to know. But I do know now. Guys should either learn to lie better or just keep their dicks inside their pants.'

'What did you do?'

'Nothing.'

'Hurt?' I asked.

She told me she was crushed. 'He's there in Canada and I'm here. I think it was my fault I thought this could work. But love is different from lust, isn't it? I mean even if he makes out with someone else, he can still be in love with me, right?'

'Yes. Probably.'

Malini told me that she first met Samarth on a summer camp when he was a freckled, frail teenager. They kept in touch and he grew into a buff, strong guy, and she, into a womanly girl. They had to be together, she said wistfully while playing with her fries, her voice devoid of sarcasm. I saw the love-struck side of her, which was adorable yet out of place. No matter how much she tried to show how tough and brave she was from the outside, from the inside, she was soft and mushy, like melted vanilla ice cream.

28

'Where were you? I have been calling you since fucking eternity,' Shashank asked.

'With Malini. Where else?' quipped Mittal. 'I told you that you will get over Avantika. Malini isn't a bad choice, Deb.'

'I'm not over her.'

He shut up. I couldn't recall the last time Mittal had not thought from his dick. I did not blame him though; he reminded me of a caricatured old *me*, with a little more hormones raging in his veins and his pants.

'What's going on with Malini?' asked Shashank, in a gruff tone. It seemed as if it was his responsibility to take care that I didn't screw up anything I had with Avantika.

'Nothing,' I said.

'He wants to bang her,' Mittal said. He lit a cigarette, took a long drag, and blew it from his nostrils, eyes closed as if meditating. 'That's what every guy wants to do with her.'

'. . . I have to keep myself occupied,' I said.

'Deb needs to keep his dick occupied,' retorted Mittal.

'Mittal, will you please shut the fuck up?' Shashank said angrily.

'If you say so . . . but just remember, it is all about sex,' he said and walked out of the room. We could hear a 'hello' in the background. He was on the phone again.

Shashank continued, 'Now, what is the matter? Tell me. Why Malini? Are you trying to make Avantika jealous?'

'Part of it, yes.'

'It's a stupid plan, Deb,' said Shashank, furiously tapping on his laptop. He was days behind on an assignment that he had asked Mittal and me to do, but we couldn't make head or tail of it.

'It makes my days easier,' I said. 'Besides, she is with Kabir.'

'It's still a stupid plan.'

I did not want to talk about it; it was already hard enough not to think about her. Frankly, I had had enough of advice from people who had never been in a relationship before.

In a split second, Shashank went from my relationship troubles to shouting at me for not attending the organizational behaviour classes. The professor took class participation seriously and gave a hard time to whoever missed his classes. Shashank said I had exhausted all my allowed leave and I should go prepared to his next class. As always, he had marked whatever I needed to study for the next class and told me he would personally ask me questions from it.

I browsed through the chapter, and nothing really made sense so I crammed it all up. Mittal left the course midway, saying that the professor would call me for the presentation, not him, since I was the notorious absentee. Management education is like being in an army camp with unfit, non-charming, ridiculous-looking jug heads. Deadlines are sacrosanct and absenteeism is looked down upon. The first battle lines of the corporate world are drawn in the management campuses itself; everyone's looking over their shoulders, wondering if they would be the ones laid off after ten years in the company that decides it needs to cut down and hire young blood and outside candidates.

Mittal slept and I revised the chapter.

29

Subir Verma was probably the smartest professor in MDI; he was also the most self-aware. He was known for his mercurial temper, and many students had borne the brunt of the red pen which he used with much brutality on the answer sheets of his least favourite students. He was known to dock peoples' placements on a whim. Other than that, he was a cool guy when he was in a good mood, and often regaled us with stories about businesses he had turned on their heads working as a consultant.

My hopes were dashed when he banged the door shut from inside even though he was a few minutes before time. He took the attendance like a drill sergeant and his eyes stayed for more than a few seconds on me, probably because of the 'A' marks on the attendance sheet. He had spotted my absence in class as Shashank had said he would. I gulped.

'Deb, to the board,' he said as he walked up the stairs of the class. 'Show me the slides.'

I put the pen drive in and clicked on the icon. The slides Shashank had prepared for me showed up on the projector screen, white and green and complete with data and analysis of a company that made diapers for old men and women.

'Start,' he said.

'. . . the company was named Acme Diapers, where Acme retained the original management style . . .' I started reading from the slides.

'What? What did you just say?' he bellowed.

'Sir . . . original . . . original management . . .'

'Sixth semester . . . and this is what you say? Original? You're an engineer, aren't you?' he asked.

'Yes, sir, mechanical engineer . . .'

He resumed the shouting, 'I figured that out, son. Just because you have paid the fees does not mean I am obliged to listen to your garbage and suffer you. Give me the goddamned word for the organization. For Acme Diapers! NOW!'

'Sir, Omega was a flat organization, whereas Acme was a tall organization with more hierarchy . . .'

'What kind of class am I holding here? Is this an English class or an organizational behaviour class? You are going to be a God darn manager, Deb. Use words like they mean something. The company was a world leader for diapers for adults. Give them the courtesy at least.'

'Sir, Acme is more horizontally differentiated . . . Omega is not, but the power is more decentralized . . .' I spoke for a few minutes and sprinkled as much jargon as I could, shocked at the amount of senseless terms I had retained in the past year.

'What crap are you talking, Deb?' he shouted out again.

'Give me that word. Or you get a minus ten in class participation. NOW,' grumbled Subir Verma, famous for marking students in negative. 'Leave the class if you don't know. Leave the class right now!'

I stood there and stared blankly at the professor. With every second I could see my grades slipping. A, A-, B, B- . . . nope, definitely a D-. He shouted again and I felt the ground slipping away from beneath my feet, my head spun, and I could feel tears welling up behind my eyes.

'Did you not hear me? Give me the terms, or get out of the class. Don't just look down and stand there like a dumb donkey,' said Subir Verma.

I looked up, embarrassed, angry and broken, and saw Avantika staring right at me from three benches away. She was trying to tell me something. She mouthed something, her lips moved. I followed her lips as I had done so many times in the past.

'Sir. O-o-o-rganic . . . and . . . umm . . . e-e-e . . .' Avantika gave me a thumbs up and smiled and mouthed the words even more clearly for me to follow. 'Mechanistic?'

I felt students sighing, vicariously enjoying the defeat of the tyrannical professor, united in my victory.

'FINALLY. That's right! Go back to your seat. Kanika? To the board.'

I went to my seat, smiling and slightly relieved. Avantika was marking her book, flipping pages, like nothing had happened. It was our first contact in a month, and I felt like I had been underwater, out of breath, dying, all this time.

'Avantika?' asked Shashank.

I nodded my head.

~

'It was Avantika, right?' asked Malini as we sat down for lunch.

'Yes.'

'So, you are going to talk to her?' asked Malini, crunching the half-sodden poppadum in her mouth, cringing.

'Yes.'

'When? Do it now!' exclaimed Malini.

'I will call her tonight.'

Now that she had sort of responded, I was at ease. At least I was not getting paranoid now. Things would be fine now. *After all, she smiled at me in the class*, I said to myself. Sooner or later. Better sooner than later.

~

There was still no answer. The phone rang till a woman from Vodafone told me politely to call the user later; maybe there was a message in that.

I was underwater and dying again. Maybe what happened in the class was just out of pity of seeing me stand there and get slaughtered by a Hitler-esque professor. She wasn't online; my staring at her name didn't make the red icon on the left of her name glow. Everyone said things would be okay, and it rarely means anything, but I still believed in it.

When? When? When?

I sat down on the corner of the bed with the phone in my hand, and scrolled through all the pictures we had clicked together, wondering if she ever did the same. We were so fucking happy.

Crying came naturally to me those days; I could cry into the night, cry in the morning till I got to class, cry while walking back to my bed, bury myself into the mattress and cry some more. It seemed so pointless that I was killing myself over someone who did not even care what was happening to me.

There was a loud knock on the door and I was half sure it was Mittal. Half-heartedly I pulled myself up, put on a T-shirt, torn near the armpits, and unlocked the door.

'Avantika?' I asked, almost immediately aware of my red eyes, the unshaved beard, the torn T-shirt, and in general, my unhandsome face.

'I missed you,' said Avantika and threw her arms around me.

30

I took her by her hand and closed the door behind her. It didn't look like she had cried for her almond-shaped dark eyes were still clear, but her face had a strange melancholy, like she was hiding something, but I could very well be imagining it.

'I missed you too,' I said. It sounded stupid and inadequate and I felt like there was lexical gap in the *Oxford English Dictionary* because 'missing' her didn't cover the tip of how I felt.

'Baby,' she said and I found both of us crying profusely in her embrace. Which only got tighter with us crying harder. Guilt swept over me, but I also felt relieved. I wished that I had a time machine so that I could go back in time and make everything all right for her. The corridors felt silent and the crickets were on to their jobs, and we were still sitting on the bed, hugging each other.

'Why did you go?' I asked her.

'I needed time.'

'Please don't do it again.' I kissed her.

'I will try not to.'

I wanted to ask her about Kabir, but I did not want to spoil the moment. Though the topic kept pricking me from the inside, like my heart suddenly had turned into a porcupine in its excited state.

'You're hanging out a lot with Malini?' asked Avantika, half-joking, a whole lot annoyed.

'Oh . . . you noticed?'

'What were you thinking? Wasn't I supposed to?'

'Yes, you were. The only reason why I was with her was because I wanted to catch your attention,' I said. 'You seemed so distant and aloof. What was I supposed to do?'

'You succeeded,' she said.

'All I want is you, Avantika. I am so sorry,' I said.

'. . .'

'. . .'

'I missed you so much.'

'I missed you too.'

'Am I forgiven?' I asked her.

After a few seconds of deathly cold silence, she said, 'Deb . . .'

'Yes?'

'I love you. So much that it scares me,' she said.

'What do you mean?'

'I should have been angry at you that you kissed her. I was . . . but only for a short while. I had forgiven you even before we reached college,' said Avantika, tears streaking down her cheeks.

'You had? Then why did you need time?' I asked.

'I just got scared that I had forgiven you so easily. How could I love you so much? I mean . . . What if you leave me some day? What will happen to me then, Deb? What if you just decide to go and never come back? What if I wrong you some day and you're unable to forgive me? What happens then?'

'I will never leave you . . .'

'That's what you said the last time . . . and you kissed her,' she said.

I had nothing to say and I hung my head in shame, waiting for the earth to open up and swallow me whole. The power of her love for me always made me feel insignificant.

We just talked that night, and periodically, we broke down more than once. She told me how hard it was for her to get Malini out of her head. It was tougher for her than it was for me, she said. She told me that she had spent the last few weeks crying to sleep every day; and that my countless messages gave her the strength to go through the days or it would have been a lot tougher for her. I was glad that I had not stopped texting her. It is always tougher for a girl, she said.

'You didn't miss me as much as I did, did you?' I asked.

'I did.'

'Why? Kabir wasn't as interesting?' I do not know why on earth I was taking his name repeatedly for it pained like a bitch.

She turned my head and kissed me, 'No one can replace you, baby,' she said. 'You are the best.' She went on to tell me that he was not as funny or as interesting as I was. My grin kept widening with every passing second.

'Thank you.'

'. . . and you owe me a treat, Deb . . . a big one.'

'And why is that?'

'Subir Verma? Strikes a bell?'

'Yes, for that, you deserve one . . . should we call Kabir too?'

'Deb? Can you stop with Kabir? Enough.'

'Sure. Sorry.'

'I can talk about Malini and you, too, you know. That's all I thought about in the past so many days,' she said.

I did not debate that. I had been unfair to her. A few days later, I came across a few poems she had written in that period and every one of them was more painful than the previous one. Not a day has gone since, when I haven't regretted what I had done to her.

~

The next few days I followed Avantika like a shadow—never let her out of sight, and showered her with surprises every few hours, tried out every cheesy line I could have come up with or heard somewhere, and tried to do my best to be funny and charming and spontaneous. I wanted her to be so incredibly happy that she would never think of leaving me again. Had I had more money, I would have changed her entire wardrobe in a matter of weeks. I was broke by the time she knocked sense into my head and asked me to stop buying her things that she didn't need.

Those days, it was hard to wipe that huge grin off my face. It was just like the old times. Life was complete again, and I was falling in love all over again, for the millionth time, with the same girl, for the same little charming things she did.

'You really are wooing me all over again,' said Avantika. 'I can get used to this. This will be our new working standard. Anything less and I would be seriously disappointed.'

'I will make sure that doesn't happen,' I answered.

'Deb . . . you don't have to do it again. I am already yours,' she smiled lovingly.

'I wouldn't really mind doing it again. I'm not doing it for you. I'm doing it for myself.' I leaned into her and rubbed my nose on her neck and she slapped me away.

'Behave. This is a class!'

'So? You really have gotten old and boring! Remember? Last year?'

It was in December, I remembered. She had challenged me that I could not get a CGPA in excess of seven, which was a daunting task, bordering on the impossible. When I got a 7.08, it was payback time. We had made out in the dean's office. I had jumped out of the window, just in time before the dean walked in and wondered if a cat had vandalized his table.

Mittal entered the class late and sat next to us, grinning wildly. 'I told you she will be back,' Mittal said.

'Mittal, had it been up to you, you would have made him sleep with Malini,' Avantika butted in.

'I would have. Most certainly. But it wouldn't have mattered to you, Avantika. You would have still forgiven him and taken him back. That's what girls do. They forgive, but they never forget. Guys, on the other hand, don't do either.'

Avantika shrugged and held my hand under the table. 'Whatever.'

'Is it? Kiss me, Avantika,' said Mittal, 'and let's see if Deb forgives you and accepts you.'

'I would rather die,' Avantika remarked.

No one said a word for a while; Mittal's words hung like a smokescreen between us; Avantika fiddled with her pencil, her grip on my hand loosening.

Mittal broke the silence, 'Anyway, since now you are off Malini—'

'I was never on her!' I protested.

'Whatever. But since you two are together again, I guess I have a chance with Malini again. I think we had fun the other day. We drank, we smoked some weed and we talked. She's really nice, a little rude and upfront, but nice,' he said.

'I agree. Why can't you stick to one?' asked Avantika.

'What's the use?' asked Mittal. 'And frankly speaking, I have seen so many girls cheat on their boyfriends that I can't trust anyone. I don't want some guy to come and fuck over my relationship and make me feel worthless about it. I would rather be the guy girls cheat on with rather than the guy whom they cheat.'

'Some day you will have to let go,' Avantika said.

Someone's phone beeped and all eyes turned towards Mittal's, including the professor's, and he looked down at his phone. He said 'Mom' and walked out of the class.

'That wasn't his mom,' Avantika said.

'I don't think so.'

31

Midterms were just two days away now, and it was just in time that Avantika and I had patched up again. The only good thing about a break-up is that the patch-up sex is always great. So is the patch-up love, the patch-up gifts, the patch-up moments, the patch-up tears. They all make up for all the time lost during the break-up. Whenever the time you were away from that person flashes in front of your eyes, it just makes you love the person even more.

'Will you stop staring and concentrate on the book?' said Avantika, with a smile. 'And no, I don't mind you doing that, but you are distracting me.'

'I am sorry for that,' I said and tried to make sense of the graphs in my books which were alive, like earthworms, and their patterns were beyond my understanding. Her phone rang again, for the tenth time that day.

'Hey . . . My room . . . Yes, he is here too . . . No, I will be here . . . How much have you done? . . . Best of luck . . . C'mon, you will do it . . . You always do . . . Yeah . . . Yeah . . . Ha ha! . . . Why not? . . . No . . . Yeah . . . Later . . . Bye . . .'

God knows I tried, but I couldn't help myself from asking, 'Kabir?'

'Yes.'

'And this is not distracting?'

'I didn't call him,' said Avantika, her eyes asking me to shut up. I did exactly that. I tried hard to concentrate, but all I could do was to relive the conversation again.

'He is here too.'

Does he want to come here?

'I will be here.'

He has asked her to come out?

'No . . . Yeah . . . Later . . . Bye'

She said no to what? What did he ask? I tried to frame as many questions as possible to it and each one made my insides squirm in disgust.

Say you love me? No.

But you do, right? Yeah.

Then, say it. Later . . . Bye.

I wanted to check her dialled calls, received calls and inbox, but then I checked myself for I knew I was being paranoid. She was still taking notes in a small diary. She looked at me, smiled and got back to brand management. A few hours passed.

'How much have you done?' she asked and I told her the page number I was on.

'What the hell are you doing?' asked Avantika and called me over. 'Is there something wrong?'

'No. I just love you,' I said.

She smiled and took the book from me. 'That is a nice thing to say and you can say it over and over again till your tongue's paralysed, and then say it again, but that is no excuse for not studying.'

She flipped through the pages and started to explain each topic to me, took care that I listened to every word that she said and I understood everything. She probably used more time in explaining everything than she had taken in studying everything herself. She would make a great teacher, I remember thinking to myself at the time.

'That is all I have done till now,' she said, tired from all the explaining.

'You are the best teacher, ever.'

'Only for you, baby,' she pulled my cheeks and kissed them.

'I am glad.'

'You want to stay here? Or go back to your room?'

It was two in the night, and I wasn't supposed to be in the girls' hostel.

'Is that even a valid question?'

'Not really.'

It wasn't until the early hours of the next morning that we finished the course and post that we lay next to each other; her touch still got my nerves to tingle, and then we made love, tired yet fulfilling.

'Isn't it so strange that even after three years, I can't keep my hands off you?' I said.

'Not really. I like to believe that I am incredibly good-looking even after all these years.' She winked.

'Yeah. That is true, too.'

'You're sweet,' said Avantika and pulled hard at my cheeks. 'I think it's because we are still in love with each other.'

I nodded. 'What's love to you?' I asked. My mind went off to when Malini had asked me the question and I had replied that love for me was Avantika. For me it was a simple answer to a simple question. But Avantika was a girl, and females have a convoluted answer to every question, no matter how straightforward it is.

'Love is conversation.'

'Conversation? Are you trying to be intelligent?' I smirked.

'Firstly, I am intelligent, and second, no, it is just something that I feel.'

'I don't want to come across as stupid, but I don't get it.'

'Look, Deb, right now, we are into all this, you know, trying to take each other down, getting our hands in all the strange tingly places all the time, but with time it will all go. You will start using Viagra; I will not be thin or hot or anything. Sex won't be as much fun as it is right now.'

'They have Botox and slimming packages. We can start investing right now.'

'Shut up, Deb. That's not the point. The point is that we will still be together, and not for this. The only thing left then would be what we have to say to each other. People's hips give way, they lose their teeth and they are still in love. And they are definitely not having sex, or going to parties any more. They talk. The only thing that remains is conversation. That is all that will remain.'

'You have a point there.'

'So, what is lust?' I asked. I really had no interest in the conversation, I just really wanted to hug and sleep tight. Making love to Avantika was always intense; it was like she had been raised by wolves.

'Lust is lust! It's what we feel after the first kiss . . .' She smirked.

'And it has nothing to do with love?'

'Yeah . . . pretty much,' she said.

'But how do you get to the lust part if the love part, that is the first kiss part, doesn't happen?'

'Don't get into technicalities now,' she said.

' . . . '

' . . . '

We set the alarm clock to fifteen minutes before the exam time, and slept. I dreamt vividly of a time when we would be talking to each other, endlessly, slurring in our toothless speech.

32

'How did it go?' asked Avantika, smiling.
'As if you don't know.' I winked.

We had cheated. At the one-hour mark, Avantika and I had met at the water cooler and she had dictated the answers to the questions I hadn't cracked. It was a ritual for us. It had started with the first exam we took at MDI, and that's what we did in every exam thereafter. A few people had caught us on various occasions, but Avantika was too smart, and too good-looking to be indicted in a cheating case.

'What plans tomorrow?' I asked. It was the last exam and, as it happens, one just stops giving a damn—however, not Avantika, who treated it as seriously as any other exam.

'We decide tomorrow?' she said sternly.

'Okay.'

Kabir passed us as we walked to our own rooms to catch a little sleep. He smiled at Avantika and she smiled back. Kabir used to sit right in front of Avantika and they had quite a lot to chat about just before the exam. They were neck to neck till the last semester but Kabir now had a healthy lead of 0.2 grade points over Avantika. That smug, brilliant bastard.

'How did his exam go?' I asked her.

'What do you expect? He is Kabir.' She sighed, surely thinking of whether she would be able to beat him and obliterate his lead. 'Now go sleep, Deb. See you in the evening. And no touching today. We screw up the last paper every time.'

'Cross my heart and hope to die.'

'We will see.'

33

'Hey.' I swung open the door and it banged on the wall of Avantika's room.

'Shhh . . .' She put a finger on my lips.

Avantika was on the phone and talking very formally to a heavy male voice on the other side of the phone. She talked about financials, return on investments, portfolios, the kind of stuff I knew nothing about. I sat in the corner waiting for the awesomely boring conversation to stop clawing at my brain. Fifteen minutes passed and she was still yakking on the phone and now discussed every mundane detail about MDI. I logged into her Gmail chats and started reading her chats.

Chat with Deb. (250 lines)
Chat with Deb. (323 lines)
Chat with Deb. (298 lines)
Chat with Kabir. (150 lines)
Chat with Kabir. (50 lines)
Chat with Deb. (345 lines)

Curious and jealous, I clicked on her chats with Kabir. My heart pounded. They talked about nothing controversial. Their chats revolved around classes, careers and projects. Harmless. I sighed. There was nothing that offended me. Kabir had called her 'baby' a few times, but he called every girl that. So . . . it was harmless. I felt a little bad since I had checked her chats; we never shared passwords to our mail IDs or social-networking accounts.

'What are you doing?' she asked. I hadn't noticed that she had disconnected the call.

'Nothing.'

'Deb? Reading my chats? How rude!' she said and closed the window.

'Why? You have something to hide?'

'No. I do not. But if there would have been something to tell you, I would have told you by now. And if I have not, then probably I don't want you to know. Get it?' she said. She spoke so quickly, that all I could make out were her bright pink lips moving. And that in itself was not that bad a sight.

'In short does that mean you want to make out right now, right here?'

'Very funny,' she said. 'By the way, where is your book?'

'Book? What book? Easy one tomorrow. Just go through it once and tell me what's in there,' I said. 'Last exams are not meant to be studied for, everyone knows that, right? It's also in the student handbook, I think.'

'I am so not going to do that. You know I can't concentrate with you sitting there doing nothing.'

'I will sit here and read something else. That should work, right?'

'Maybe.'

'GREAT. Oh, whose call was it?' I asked her.

'Kabir's father is floating a live project in MDI. And we are doing it together. It's a little tough but I think we will manage between ourselves.'

'What? Ourselves? Ourselves as in? You and Kabir?'

'No, just you and me. Kabir is just getting the project floated in our college. This project would look good on our résumés,' explained Avantika.

'I am not interested,' I said.

'What? Don't be silly, Deb. It isn't for me. I already have a placement. I don't need it. It will be good for you. And since I am in it, you don't even have to work for it.'

'I don't want to have to do anything with him. I hate him and I'm not doing anything for his father,' I snapped.

'Baby, I know you don't like him, but this is for your own good,' she said.

'I don't want it. Period.'

'Can we talk about it later?'

'There is nothing to talk about. If you want to do it, go ahead,' I said angrily.

'I just wanted it for you,' she said; her mood dipped and shoulders slumped. She started marking her book, while I lay in the corner, fuming. The whole Kabir thing was driving me crazy. I knew she was mine, but I could not help it. I sat there telling myself that she was mine, no matter what came her way. Thinking like that helped—a little. I did not study much that day. Avantika taught me a little and I don't remember how the exam went.

We never did that live project. It was foolish of me, and as usual, jealousy got the better of me.

I was always the possessive, angry boyfriend.

34

'Sad crowd!' I shouted in her ear, her eyes glued to the big projector screen, which covered half the wall in front of us. The screen was hazy and not really great. It was Liverpool vs Arsenal. She was an Arsenal fan, and it would be over her dead body that she would ever miss a match. I wasn't a big fan—neither of the game nor of the team. Her ex-boyfriend was an Arsenal fan and she had got this obsession from there, a part of her I'm not sure I liked very much.

'Shut up,' said Avantika, and stuffed her mouth with the fried burrito she had ordered and washed it down with a tall tumbler of iced tea. The score line was tied and, from the little I knew of football, it was a tight match between evenly matched players—all of them with enviable bodies, waiting to be showed off to the boisterous, zombie-like crowd and the cameras after a sensational goal. I dared not disturb her. The last time I made fun of an Arsenal player, she didn't let me touch her for a week.

'Fu—' she stopped herself from shouting aloud as the Liverpool goalie made a valiant save just before half-time.

'Liverpool is going to suck them out in the next half,' a guy in a Liverpool T-shirt said out loud. It was aimed at Avantika. I put my hand over Avantika to calm her down as she puffed like a bull marking a matador waving a red flag at her. Last year she had thrown an ashtray at a guy who said Arsenal was full of 'pussies and unnecessarily expensive players'; we were thrown out of the place. This time she let the guy go with just a subtle expression of displeasure—the middle finger. He reciprocated with a more vulgar rendition of the same.

'I so want to knock the head off that guy,' she said.

'Calm down. Just a game!'

'Deb, this is the last time I am telling you. It is not JUST A GAME!'

'Fine. It is a religion.'

'Good,' she said.

'Hold this.' She gave me her handbag. 'I will just be back from the washroom.'

She asked the waiter where the washroom was and I imagined her smashing the mirror in anger. The half-time analysis ended, the match started again and I could hear shouts of ecstasy and anguish. Avantika took more time than usual; she hated to miss the first few minutes after half-time—the time most prone to slip-ups. I called her and her phone rang in her handbag. I took the phone out and started to fiddle with it, bored with the match proceedings.

The sounds dimmed as I flicked through her cell phone, through the picture gallery, and then, the text messages in her phone; the shouts drowned out, and I could hear myself screaming, loud and silent at the same time. My hands clenched around the phone as I stared at the picture of Kabir and Avantika, with Kabir's arm around her and Avantika looking at him lovingly while she clicked the self-taken picture. It took them five attempts to get the picture right and the failed attempts were in her phone too; and in all of them Kabir's arm was around her and she was looking at him, unblinking and happy. The text on the same date from Kabir said, 'I wonder why I didn't find you earlier,' and Avantika had replied with a smiley face and a heart smiley.

It felt like someone had punched me hard in the guts, and I puked them from my mouth. My stomach churned, my head spun and blood rushed to my face. I got up from my chair, paced around my table and waited for her. I wished I had not looked into her cell phone. I tried hard to calm myself down. I sat down, opened that picture and kept the phone on the table.

'You look . . . strange,' said Avantika, as she walked up to me, smiling.

'What's this?' I said and pushed the phone in her hands.

'What?'

'The message! What is that? Care to explain, Avantika? The pictures?'

'It's nothing . . .' she stuttered.

To see her stutter just deepened my suspicion. I was losing my head. It was not the picture, but the smile, the loving gaze that hurt me more.

'When was this . . . tell me . . . Please tell me, Avantika,' I said, barely keeping myself from shouting.

The guy from the other table shouted 'SLUT' to his friends. I looked at him and he looked away.

'I . . . Can we go?' she asked.

'Go? Where?'

'Can we just go back to college? Will explain there?' she said.

I picked up my things and we left the place. I strode down to the car, leaving her far behind. I fumed while I waited for her to come to the car. The car whizzed dangerously through the narrow lanes as I pushed the pedal as far as it could go. A few people escaped from being crushed beneath the wheel, jumping out of the way just in time.

'Calm down,' she said.

'Calm down? After seeing this? How the fuck can you let any guy talk to you like that? And Kabir? I was there killing myself after you left me and this is what you were up to.'

'Deb . . .'

'You were smiling and taking pictures and getting all mushy with him! You were storing it for posterity? Your sweetheart and you? There are not one or two but five pictures,' I grumbled and the old, decrepit engine moaned.

She put her hand on my shoulder and I shrugged it off. 'Can we just talk about it?'

'We are TALKING about it!' I shouted and parked the car with a screech outside the hostel. I muttered to myself, but I'm sure she heard it because I intended her to, 'I think we are over.'

35

We were in her room again.

'TALK,' I shouted.

'There is something I need to tell you,' she said.

'What?'

Now that she had something to tell, I really wished she had nothing to tell. I prayed and hoped there would be no story behind those pictures and the offhand message.

'I kissed him,' she said feebly.

I wished she had never told me that; I wished I hadn't heard it because I felt my world crumbling. It broke into small, tiny pieces beyond repair; it lay in front of me, broken and ridiculous and hopeless. I wished she had lied. The last few days had been good, why did she have to tell me? She could have just buried that deep inside and we could have gone on with our lives.

It didn't sink in. I asked again, hoping she would tell me she was kidding. 'You did WHAT?'

'I kissed him.'

I breathed deeply, taking care I didn't pass out on the floor. 'When? How? Why? Tell me EVERYTHING. NOW.' I was crying now—angry, betrayed and in tears.

'We went out one day . . .'

'TELL me the FUCKING date, Avantika.'

'12th October.'

'So this is what you were goddamn doing when I was not there? Kissing other people and marking the dates on the calendar. Who else did you kiss?'

'I was a little drunk.'

'Little drunk? We know you do not fucking get drunk, Avantika.'

'I am sorry.'

'Sorry? What is it? Oh. WAIT. You got bored of me, didn't you? You were just looking for a break, weren't you? Malini just gave you that chance, didn't she?'

'It's—'

'You just kissed once?'

'Yes.'

'Was he a good kisser? Was he?' I said, and paced around the room. My head started to burst. I clenched my fist and wanted to hit something, maybe Kabir, maybe her, maybe myself.

She shook her head. 'Don't ask me that.'

'DON'T ASK ME THAT? What does that mean? He was good, right? Why don't you fucking tell me? What else did you do?'

'Nothing.'

'Nothing? I don't believe you! You fucking slept with him, didn't you?' I accused her. 'I always knew there was something going on between the two of you. The question is WHY DIDN'T YOU TELL ME BEFORE THAT YOU LIKED HIM?'

'I didn't,' said Avantika, burying her face in her palms.

'You *fucking* took two years to get over your previous guy and this is how long you take to get over me? A week passes and you're already sleeping with someone else?'

'I wasn't trying to get over you,' said Avantika, now crying, her shoulders jerking, her body quivering.

'Then what the fuck was it? What the fuck was it? Swear on me you didn't do anything beyond the kiss?'

'Deb!'

'Just do it.'

'I swear.'

I threw her phone against the wall. 'Say the whole thing, Avantika.'

'I swear nothing happened beyond the kiss, Deb. Don't make me do this.'

'Was he nice? Better than me?'

'Don't ask me that, Deb,' she said. She had slumped to the ground and she put her head between her knees.

'Why? Why the fuck not! I can fucking ask you anything,' I shouted. 'You're answerable to me. You're responsible for this mess. You're responsible for me, damn it.'

'I was drunk and I don't remember how the kiss was,' she cried. 'For heavens' sake, don't do this.'

'I will. I fucking will. So how was it? Huh? HOW WAS IT? Did you like the touch of his skin against yours? Did you want him next to you?' I taunted her and I wasn't sure whether I intended to hurt her or hurt myself.

'It was different,' whimpered Avantika, still sitting on the floor, crying.

'Different?'

'I don't know, Deb. I was drunk and frustrated. It just happened. It just happened.'

'You were getting back at me by kissing that son of a bitch? Or did you always like him? You did, didn't you? That bastard always had a hard-on for you for as long as I can remember and you just gave into the temptation the first chance you got.'

'But . . .'

'Go to hell, Avantika! Go! Sleep with him. I do not fucking care. I am ending this . . . right now, right here! I don't want to see your face ever again. I can't even see you right now, Avantika. You disgust me. You know what? Mittal was right. I should have listened to him when he said it's better to be the guy who sleeps with girlfriends of other guys, than be the boyfriend who gets cheated on. Malini is so much better than you. Just GO AWAY, Avantika.'

'But, Deb . . .'

'I don't want you in my life. Go and sleep with him. Why did you come back, Avantika? To hurt me?' I said and walked towards her. 'Mittal was right. I should look beyond you. You are a waste of time. You're a fucking waste of time.'

I slammed the door as I left. I felt like crying aloud and banging my head on the wall till it split open—do something that would make the hurt go away. I wished she would cry behind the door I had just closed on her; I wished she would suffer; I wished she would miss me and never be loved like I loved her; I wished she were dead. I texted her the last part.

36

I had two options. Option one was go to Kabir's room, tie him to a chair, slowly pull out his fingernails and toenails one by one, break his ribs and get everyone who hated him to piss on him. And then I wanted him to kill himself.

Second, I could go into Malini's room and sleep with her. Avantika had been a slut, and I could be too. I knew I had kissed Malini but it was a mistake, a drunken mistake. She should have tried to make things better, not go and kiss another guy, more so the guy I hated with all my heart.

I texted Avantika instead.

Drunk? You bloody took a picture after it!

Deb, I am really sorry, it meant nothing.
It was different, right? He was better, I am sure
Why don't you go to him? I won't be messaging
you from now on. Bye, baby. Take care.

I am sorry. Nobody makes me feel the way you do.
I did not even feel like kissing somebody. I don't
even care how it was. It really meant nothing. It
felt nothing.

Didn't you feel guilty?

It killed me. It still is.

That is why you still hung out with him even
after it happened? Bullshit. Just go away,
Avantika. Isn't he seeing someone?

                              No, he broke up a month back.
So you were celebrating your break-ups! Nice!
Is that why you kissed him? You were waiting
for him to break up or what?

                              It's nothing like that, Deb.
I know nothing about you. You didn't miss me.
You were kissing him. Please don't message
me after this. I won't. Bye.

I threw my phone away from me, and held my bursting
head, cursing her for having made it worse. I thought of talking
about it to Malini, Shashank . . . or Mittal but it felt so wrong
telling them. No one needed to know Avantika had kissed
someone else; it wasn't their business to know.

Kabir and Avantika kissing.

How would I ever get that image out of my head? I
talked to myself the entire night, trying to think like her,
think like me, advocate both sides and do something to
soothe myself. No matter how hard I tried, I could not stop
it from hurting.

She was just alone, and frustrated, tired of my immaturity.
There have been times when you have wanted to kiss Malini again,
haven't you?

No, I have not. They were just passing thoughts.

No, they weren't. That was just because you wanted to feel a
little different, a little better. So what if she did?

But she kissed him. I didn't kiss Malini.

But you wanted to.

But I didn't, that is the point. She did and she didn't even feel
guilty about it. She was still talking to him after it. How can she

do that? Didn't she feel guilty? Didn't she think what it could do to our relationship?

How can she lie so blatantly? I fucking told her the moment I came from Mumbai about what happened. How can she not tell me? So many days passed? How can she not? I was not even in my senses when that fucking happened. She is such a . . . . No, she is not . . . She did everything for me. Things that I wouldn't do for her. But why this? Was she getting bored? Why did they take pictures?

I can't see him. I can't see her. How can I possibly see her walking around with him? Or how can I just see Kabir? That bastard! Strutting around, feeling good about himself. He kissed the girl I was dating. He must be laughing behind my back, calling me impotent, less of a man, and what not.

But is it his fault?

Not really.

Who wouldn't kiss her? Who wouldn't want to kiss her? Fuck man . . . What the fuck should I do? I want her. I so want her right now. I wish she would just hug me and tell me that everything will be fine. And tell me that I was better. Tell me that she missed me.

I had to forgive her; she had forgiven me too. I was just being revengeful and sadistic and foolish and, in general, a pig. I still loved her, and she still loved me. I had to go back to her. I just had to. I could not let Kabir come between us.

I called her up.

37

'Hi,' I called her up.

'Hi, Deb. What are you doing?' she asked.

'Nothing. Was reading the newspaper and I don't remember the last time I read it.' We weren't very good at small talk; our relationship had started with a random kiss and since then we had never talked about the latest movies we had watched or the weather or exam schedules.

'I know about that, Deb,' she said.

'Look, Avantika ... despite what you told me, despite what happened, I have missed you. The past few hours have been quite traumatic, to put it lightly. I have never felt more suicidal. I just want you back. I miss you ...'

'I missed you too ... and I am sorry about what happened. I really am,' she said, still crying.

'I know, Avantika. It's just that it's hard not to think about it.'

'I know, Deb ...'

'I am sorry for acting so immaturely, Avantika. I should have understood. I mean even I kissed Malini and you understood. I am sorry for being such an ass.'

'Is that why you have forgiven me? Because I forgave you for kissing Malini? Is that why you think you should come

156

back to me? Because you kissed her and I kissed him and that makes it all okay?' she asked.

'I just understand. I love you too much to leave you like that. It would be foolish and unfair.'

'I am sorry, Deb, but I don't think we should be together.' She still silently sobbed.

'Why?' I asked.

'I don't deserve you, Deb,' she said. 'You told me everything and believed in me. You didn't hide anything from me.' She added after a pause, 'I did.'

'So-w-w-what do you mean?' I stammered.

'Nothing.'

'TELL ME. Did you hide something?'

'I lied. Yes, I did. Since you forgave me because we both had kissed someone else, I don't think you're going to forgive me for what I didn't tell you.'

The pain came rushing back and my head pounded like it was imploding inside. 'What? What did you lie about?' I asked.

'I don't want to hurt you any more,' she said. 'You should just leave me.'

'What? TELL me clearly, Avantika. Please don't play games with me,' I said.

'Kabir and I didn't stop at the kiss,' she said, her voice icy cold.

'W-what?'

'Just leave me, Deb. I slept with him. You don't deserve me. You don't have to forgive me for it.'

'Just tell me what you did with him. EVERY fucking THING,' I said, banging my fist against my forehead, crying.

'Please, Deb, just leave me. I am fine. I am sorry. We should not be together . . .'

'It is not about you. It is about me! I want to know. Tell me EVERYTHING.'

'I don't want you to know.' She was still crying. 'I don't want to hurt you more than I already have.'

'I WANT TO KNOW,' I shouted. 'What part of I WANT TO KNOW did you not get? WHAT ELSE HAPPENED?'

'Something more happened . . . Deb . . .'

'How many times did he fuck you? Just tell me. When did it happen? Where did you do it?'

'We went to his place,' she said.

'You went to his place that day? I saw you in college. I fucking saw you in college later that day. You had fucked him before that? And you swore on me . . . but you swore on me that nothing happened after the kiss. You swore?'

'I lied,' she said.

'Tell me what happened . . . when . . . please do not fuck around. I want the truth, right now. Did you guys make out more than once?' I shouted.

'Yes,' she said.

'You kissed him twice?'

'Yes,' she said.

'You're such a slut, Avantika. You're still sleeping with him, aren't you? Are you?' More than angry, I felt like dying.

'No, I'm not!'

'You are still fucking him. I just know. I just know that you are.'

'No,' she said.

'Why did you do it, Avantika? Why?'

I sat in the corner of the room, defeated and sad; I was no longer angry, just betrayed. My love had no meaning for her.

I did not know what to say to her. This was *over*. She had slept with him twice—or more, who knows. She was not drunk and it was not a mistake; they knew what they were doing,

Avantika knew that she was sleeping with him while I lay rotting in my room. Malini and I might have kissed, but this wasn't what I deserved.

'I think this is the last time we are talking, Avantika. Thank you so much for sleeping around. I never thought you would.' I found it so hard not to cry.

'I am sorry, Deb. Please don't cry.'

'You don't have to be. Why didn't you just tell me that you wanted someone better? I would have moved out of your life. I wouldn't have asked you a single question.'

'Please don't cry, Deb. I didn't mean for any of this to happen. Can you find it in your heart to forgive me?'

'Forgiveness? I hate you, Avantika. Of all the people I hate in my life, I hate you the most. You are pathetic.'

'But I promise—'

'Do you love him? Kabir?' I asked. The words felt like searing embers of coal on my tongue; the images of Kabir and Avantika naked imprinted on my mind.

'I don't love him,' she said. 'I love you.'

'Oh, so you love me and still you sleep with him? What are you, Avantika? Did he fucking pay you?'

'Deb! ENOUGH.'

'Fuck you, Avantika,' I cried out loud. I felt dead and numb. 'Nothing you say makes a difference now. You're just a whore and a liar.'

'Deb, I will always love you. I always have,' she said. 'Can't we just get past this? I promise I will make everything all right,' she begged. 'We will get past this. Can't you forgive me? For all that we have shared, can't you let this go?'

I stayed shut, and I imagined them in Kabir's hostel room, wrapped around each other, Avantika telling Kabir how good he was, how he was better than me, and Kabir saying that she deserved someone better, someone who could take care of her needs, inside the bedroom and otherwise. 'He was better than me, wasn't he?'

'Why are you asking me that? Does that matter?' She was still crying as she said that. I did not care about her tears; I cared about mine.

'It does matter. Of course, it matters. It matters. You sleep with him. Not once, but twice and you say it shouldn't matter? I want to know why you did it!'

'I am sorry, Deb.'

'Why did you come back to me? Why? He is single, and he is good in bed. Why don't you go back to him? Why don't you? Just go and make this all go away.'

'Please stop crying, Deb.'

'How many guys have you slept with in the last three years? Two? Three?'

'No, Deb, what are you talking—'

'How do I believe you?'

'Why would I lie now?'

'I don't believe a single thing you say, Avantika. You are just . . . You love him, right?'

'Please don't say that, Deb. He does nothing to me . . . I was just . . .' She was barely audible because of all the crying. And I wanted her to cry more. 'Why don't you just say it, Avantika? Why won't you say that he was better than I ever was?'

'I am not comparing an awful mistake with what I have loved the most.'

'Have a great time with him. Go. Sleep with him. I do not give a damn. Our relationship was the biggest mistake. I regret every day that I have ever spent with you. I should have never . . .'

'Listen, Deb. It was nothing. It meant nothing. You know that. I do not care what happened. Just listen to me. Nobody can make me feel like you do. That is what matters. That is all that matters,' she cried aloud. 'It was nothing. I do not want to compare anything that I had with you with anyone else. I cannot. I don't care about anything else. Can't you just forgive me?'

'You are not mine any more. You are no longer my Avantika. Just go.'

I disconnected the line and threw the cell phone across the room—it broke and the battery spilled out. The phone was dead, the screen cracked. And with that a part of me died within.

The tears stopped. My heart felt like it had been ripped out. How could I have not seen that before? Avantika always deserved someone better than me. She had finally given into the temptation. If I had a gun, I would have used it. I would have killed myself and relieved myself of the pain.

38

She sat on the first seat, alone, reading the newspaper, peering over the top of her anti-glare spectacles which she only wore to hide her reddened eyes. I took my seat in the third row. I felt no love, only anger and disgust and excruciating pain. Shashank was sitting next to me, swirling a pen between his fingers and I was thinking if I could cleanly pierce it through my heart, die a painless death.

'Another fight?' Shashank asked. He stopped swirling the pen; I would have hit the ribcage and missed and it would have been a waste.

'I broke up.'

'What? What did you do?'

'I broke up and I don't want to talk to about it.'

'So does that mean you are going to start talking to Malini again?' Mittal asked.

'I don't know.'

'Just make up your damn mind, Deb. She finally picked up my call yesterday. She even broke up with her boyfriend—a vulnerable moment for her. I don't want to miss it.' Mittal chuckled, his eyes twinkled devilishly.

'I don't know whether I am going to talk to her or not, but you stay away from her. She is a nice girl and she doesn't deserve you treating her like that. Just leave her alone if you can't be with her.'

'Relationship advice from you? You just left your girlfriend, dude. That's twice in two weeks, I think,' he retorted.

'Will you two calm down? Mittal, stay away from Malini, and, Deb, sort out your thing with Avantika,' Shashank said, and just as he asked us to stay quiet, the professor saw the three of us talking, shot us a murderous look, threatened to fling a piece of chalk our way and asked us to shut up.

I looked at Kabir. He sat just behind Avantika and tried to initiate a conversation once or twice with her, pulling her hair and poking her with a pen on her back, leaving little blue marks. I saw no reaction from her side. I felt disgusted at the mere sight of him, *that sneaky bastard*. Every few minutes, my head spun around the same topic. *Why? How? What made her do it?*

The classes were a pain. I just waited for the ordeal to end, for her to get out of my sight. But how was I supposed to get her out of my mind? How was I supposed to shut my mind and not think about her? How? I thought and struggled, and it drained me; I felt physically unwell.

Sitting there on the wooden bench, burdened by betrayal and the obvious inferiority to Kabir, I weighed my options. Dying seemed very lucrative; jumping off the building was a great option, quick and painless. Turning to alcoholism was a viable option. Making her repent for the rest of her life when she would see me dead in a ditch with a bottle in my hand would serve her right. Alcohol made me think of the girl with tiny bottles of vodka beneath her bed—Malini.

I could use a drink and I sure needed a friend. After the classes ended, I almost ran to Malini's room. Standing outside her door, I felt nervous; it had been years since I had last been single and tried to court someone other than Avantika. I ran back to my room, changed my shirt, sprayed myself with a wasteful amount of deodorant, and checked my face in the mirror. A scraggly, tired face stared back at me.

Her door was open when I got there and I closed it behind me. My face was wet, with tears and with sweat.

'You want to talk about it?' Malini said as she closed down a comic, *Batman Retold*, and threw it on the table. It landed with a loud thud.

'Yes. Maybe.'

I told her what had happened, detailing every bit, trying not to break down into tears. It surprised me how clearly I recalled every moment of it.

'Is that reason enough to leave her? That she slept with someone else? Didn't she say she was sorry?'

'I had spent a month without her before. I can live another one. And maybe another one. I can do without her,' I told her. 'You think it's easy to live with the recurring images of her making out with someone else? That someone else is Kabir. That asshole.'

'Don't you think the images of you and me kissing would be troublesome for her?'

'Yes, they would be. But I was drunk, crazy drunk, and secondly, I didn't hide it from her. She did. I was wrong. But she is more wrong. She *slept* with him.'

'There is nothing like more wrong. What's wrong is wrong. And she took you back. She was ready to forgo everything. She also apologized to you and forgave your mistake. It takes a lot of courage to do that,' Malini said, sympathizing with a girl who clearly didn't deserve it.

'She was sleeping with him all that time. Do you know what that means? While I walked around the campus like a madman, spying on her, trying to see her face, she was blowing some guy. Do you have any idea how that makes me feel about myself? Like a joke.'

'I know what it means. But revenge is not the way to go. It's your time to understand her and see this through,' she said, holding my hand.

'It is not revenge. It's easy for you to say that everything is going to be okay and optimistic bullshit like that. You wouldn't know what I'm going through.'

'I wouldn't?' asked Malini, with her eyebrows raised.

Her hostile stance made me remember her break-up with her boyfriend. I tried to say that I was sorry for her, but she said I did not need to care and asked me to skip the topic. We fell silent and I flipped mindlessly through the comic, which was brilliantly drawn, though a bit dark for me.

'So?'

'Do you have something to drink?' I asked her.

'Why?'

'Do you?' I asked sternly.

'Yes.'

She fished out a whisky and a vodka bottle from beneath her bed. I grabbed the bottle and unscrewed it like lovelorn alcoholics in the movies.

'You are not drinking from it,' she said. By the time she had said it, I had already taken a ten-second gulp from it. It was bitter.

'Here, all yours,' I said and passed on the bottle, hoping she would get drunk, kiss me, and then I would have a story for Avantika. Maybe I would even exaggerate a bit.

'I don't want to drink,' Malini said.

'Please?'

'Come. Sit here.' She pulled my hand and made me sit on the mats on the floor in the corner of the room.

'What happened?' she asked. I took another huge glug, my head spun a little. I half wondered if Kabir was in her room right then, caressing her neck, kissing her, laughing at me.

'They made out,' I said and my tear glands went into overdrive.

'But, Deb, you forgave her for kissing Kabir, didn't you?'

'She told me she had just kissed. She lied to me! Now she says they have done more and they have done it more than once. When do the lies stop?'

'But didn't she take you back after you cheated on her? You kissed me twice, didn't you?'

'I don't want to talk about it. Moreover, I just kissed you. I didn't make out or sleep with you,' I defended myself.

'Fine.' She dangled the bottle in front of me. 'This will help?'

'Yes,' I said and took another huge glug, which made me a little disoriented.

'Why are you here?' she asked.

'I like you, Malini.' The words turning to mush in my mouth, my tongue flapping around like a fish out of water.

'No, you don't,' she said.

'Yes, I do. Mittal says you are sexy. I think so too.'

'You are drunk.'

'I am?' I chuckled. 'I think we should make out. Yes, we should! And then I will tell her that I slept with you. That would be great, wouldn't it?'

'Deb, get a hold.'

'Nobody loves me.'

Her tone was stern and I could get it despite my drunken state. She asked me to get up and pulled me up.

'Where are we going?'

'Nowhere. You are going to bed,' she said and helped me up. She tried to steady my wayward steps.

'Are we making out?' I smiled stupidly at her.

'No, we are not. Just sleep here.'

'I don't want to sleep yet. Maybe we can make out just a little bit?'

'You need rest,' she said as I clambered on to the

'I need you and I am not drunk. Have you ever explored the possibility of us together? You are hot and I am ugly. It makes perfect sense. Opposites attract, Malini!'

'You should sleep.'

'I am not sleepy.'

'No, I have not considered the possibility,' she said.

'Why haven't you?'

'You are not my thing,' she said.

'You haven't seen my thing.' I smiled. 'It's a monument really.'

'Not interested,' she said.

'I was lying anyway.'

I took another huge sip from the bottle before Malini wrested it away from me. Black. Blank. Darkness.

39

I pulled the blanket over me as the morning sun poured through the curtains and pierced my eyes. My head was hurting, and I felt terrible. The bed did not feel familiar. The room did not feel the same. I wasn't in Avantika's room. I woke up, my head hurt, and my lips were dry. Malini's room, though kitschy and fun, wasn't anything like Avantika's room. Bits and pieces from last night came back to me and I felt rather stupid. The alarm clock beeped and I realized it was twelve. Straight ahead, I saw a note stuck on the mirror.

> Good Morning. Water—Table. Breakfast—Table, leave it if it gets cold. Leave the room unlocked when you leave. Don't make it look like you stayed over. Take care. I will ask Mittal for your proxy.
>
> P.S. You drink like a little girl.

I drank the water and had a bite; the eggs were cold and the water was warm but I didn't mind. I hadn't eaten well in the last few days. I washed up a little and left her room. On my way back, the same thoughts clouded my mind—Kabir and Avantika. I checked my cell phone. There were twenty messages; all of them were from Avantika. I read them one after the other. They all said the same things.

> I am sorry, Deb. You mean everything to me. You can leave me if you want to, but . . . I love you and I will always be yours. Our relationship meant everything to me. It was the only beautiful thing in my life. Try not to hate me. I love you and I will always do. I am sorry for what happened and I regret it more than anything in my life. I love you so much, Deb. Your leaving me is the worst thing that ever happened to me. You were my only family.

Though I cried, I felt no pity. She slept with someone else and a few messages would not change that. I felt so repulsed, hurt and humiliated; the sickness returned to the stomach.

I didn't attend any class that day. I waited outside the classroom after the last lecture and saw Avantika leave the class alone. Kabir left with his guys in tow, laughing. Avantika's eyes and mine met briefly; her eyes were swollen and red.

I walked right past her and hugged Malini. Avantika looked away and walked into the girls' hostel.

'Going somewhere?' Malini asked.

'To see you and thank you!' I said.

'For?'

'The breakfast, the note . . . I was a mess this morning, and last night as well.'

'Never mind,' she said. 'How are you feeling now?'

'Better. Slightly. I am sorry for being so stupid last night. I was having a hard time and I dragged you into it.'

'I understand.'

'Coffee?' I asked her.

She did not say anything and we headed to the canteen. I saw Mittal and Shashank cross us; they looked at me with questions in their eyes, and I met their eyes with no answers in mine.

'So?' she asked as she sipped on the coffee.

'How was the class?' I sighed.

'The usual. And we are supposed to talk about classes?' she said sarcastically. 'You can't run away from this. You have to deal with this.'

'Running away? I am not running away.'

'Yes. You are,' she said. 'You were going back to her when she said she just kissed. But now that she took a few clothes off and made out, you can't take her back? That's just being shallow and hypocritical.'

'Listen to me. It was different. I was not in my senses. She was and she kissed him twice. They were deliberate decisions.'

'You kissed me twice, Deb.'

'I was sloshed the first time. And I didn't lie about it,' I said.

'You haven't considered the possibility that she did it because you hurt her. She lied because she didn't want to hurt you.'

'Hurt me? Didn't she think about that when she kissed and made out with him?'

'Deb, you are such a loser.'

'Why?'

'Imagine. She made out just once. Not twice just once. Would you have taken her back?'

'Umm . . . yes . . . totally.'

I was not so sure.

'You're just a jealous, chauvinistic guy,' Malini said.

Maybe I was. But Avantika should not have made out with him.

Period.

40

'Now what?' Shashank asked.
   'Nothing. I am just taking a break from the relationship business.'

'What the hell are you doing? Placements are in a week and you are doing such stunts in your life. Don't fuck them up, man. She could have helped you way better than I can.'

He gave me a list of companies he had applied to on my behalf and a bundle of forms I had to fill up before the next day. He mailed me a file that had notes on things such as recent financial events, new marketing jargon and landmark campaigns to brush up before the placement week. He was a lifesaver and a constant reminder of my stupidity.

He kept telling me that I should be with her—at least till the placement week—but what did he know about how tough it was for me?

On my way back to my hostel room, I crossed Mittal, who was as usual on the phone; he had cupped the phone in his palms as if to whisper into it. But I was too occupied to care. I grabbed a few books from my room to prepare for the placement week. Shashank, Avantika and even Mittal had offers and didn't need to study, I had to. I concentrated hard enough to kick her out of my mind for a few moments, hard enough to bring tears to my eyes.

The evening was more productive after Malini joined me in the library and marked out the exact things that would be useful. Over the next week or so, Malini took up Avantika's role; she made herself responsible for everything I did. She made sure I studied, and I know she did well because even Shashank was impressed with the kind of preparation I had before the placement week.

~

Two weeks had passed since that day, and the hurt was still there. But the days became a little more bearable. I got placed within the first few hours of the placement week in a reputed FMCG with an enviable package and I made more enemies because of it. I spent entire days with Malini, and so that kept my mind off Avantika.

The messages, the mails and the missed calls kept pouring in to tell me how much she still loved me and cared for me. Avantika told me how hard it was for her to live without me and that she would understand if I leave her, but she hoped I would forgive her.

She forwarded me the mails and chats we had exchanged over the past three years. She reminded me of everything that had happened, everything that we had seen together, every happy moment that we had spent smiling and every sad moment we had spent in each other's arms.

'Are we never going to talk?' Avantika had called me up.

'No, Avantika,' I said, dryly.

'Can't we sort it out?' she said.

'No, we can't,' I said and cut the phone.

She cried. She mailed. She wept. I replied when I wanted

to and rejected every call of hers; sometimes I picked it up and then cut the call. It gave me a sadistic pleasure to see her go through what she had made me suffer a few weeks earlier. I was yet to see her with Kabir in college, but I figured they still met when no one was looking.

Shashank and Mittal had asked a million times what had happened between the two of us, but I could not bring myself to tell them.

'Male ego,' Malini used to tell me. *I didn't want to be a lesser man.*

'Your girlfriend goes out and makes out with someone else. Where does that leave you? It just says that you're not good enough.'

'That's nonsense.' I fumed. Though that may be a part of the reason, but I didn't tell anyone because I didn't want others to gossip about her. 'Can we stop talking about her?'

'*I* talk about her?'

'Whatever. But don't encourage my conversations from now on.'

'As you say,' she responded and we ran out of things to say to each other.

'See, we have nothing else to talk about,' she said and smiled. 'The only reason we talk is because you love Avantika and you need her in your life. You might hate her now, but you won't be able to do without her for long.'

'Whatever,' I said.

41

With a month left for college to end classes were far and few. The professors no longer cared about attendance or quizzes and made our lives a lot easier. No surprise tests. No hang-ups about attendance. No negative marking for latecomers.

Slowly and steadily, Avantika's messages took a different tone. The number of messages increased but they were no longer 'I'm-sorry-please-take-me-back' messages. They were just messages that said how much she missed me and what my love meant for her, about how much she would treasure me and all that bullshit that only girls can come up with.

She said she would always wait for me and that there would be no one, absolutely no one, who would ever be as important as I was for her. I couldn't say these messages didn't affect me. They killed me. It was not a break any more. It was a break-up. And it hurt as much as I had heard it does.

Sometimes, when the nights fell, I used to give in and decide to crawl back into her life. But the mornings used to bring back all the bitterness with them and I used to find myself filled up to the brim with hate and disgust. There were times that I desperately wanted to talk to her, but the presence of Kabir around the campus ensured that I didn't talk to her.

She had done wrong, and she deserved it. Everyone around me would have agreed. Or not. I did not care.

Late one night, tired of being without her, I called her up, and as soon as I heard her voice, my heart melted and spilled on to the floor. I nevertheless tried to be stern.

'How are you?' I asked her.

'I am fine. How are you doing?'

'I am doing okay,' I said. *I am dying without you, Avantika.*

'How did the exams go?'

'They went okay,' I said. Malini had taught me this time.

' . . . '

' . . . '

'Avantika?'

'Yes?'

'Just tell me something?'

'Say?' she said.

'Did you not think of me while you were doing it?' I tried to sound very soft even though my temper was through the roof and I could have strangled someone.

'I told you that I missed you while I was with him. I am sorry.'

'Is sorry going to work, Avantika? After all that we had seen together? This is what you give me? This?'

'Why is it so important, Deb? Can't we see through this? I'm sure we can. I'm sure we can look past this, think of how we had been together and move on.'

'See through this? What are you talking about? How am I supposed to let this go? If I go and sleep with Malini every day from now on and come back to you, would you have me back? Would you?'

'I would. It wouldn't make a difference to me, Deb. I love you and I always will. You can go sleep with anybody you want to. But if you love me, I would still take you back. That's how much I love you.'

'Is that why you broke up for a month when I kissed Malini?'

'Trust me.'

'You disgust me, Avantika. You disgust me. You were such a mistake . . .'

I disconnected the line. I knew I said what I said to hurt her and make her go through the pain that I was going through. Sometimes, the pain is so constant and deep that you learn to live with it. At certain levels, she did disgust me. I was disgusted at the fact that she was with him. I was disgusted that she lied to me. I was disgusted that I had to find out everything that she had lied about to my face.

42

'How long do you plan to stay away from her?' Malini asked.

'Fifteen more days and college will end. She will go her own way and I will have a new life. I will get over her. So, I plan to stay away from her forever.'

'Why do you want to get over her when you know you could be much better with her?'

'I am good. I am doing well. I'm doing great in fact. Like super good.'

'Is that why you had to say that four times?' She smirked.

The exams had just got over and I had done surprisingly well. Avantika had not done too great. She had done terribly in fact. Kabir was the batch topper and he would collect his fake-gold gold medal for his all-round performance over the past two years.

Fifteen more days . . . and back to the world of endless cups of coffee, horrible bosses, short weekends and horrible Mondays. Just a few formalities were all that was left of our college life. It sucked. Two years . . . gone, just like that. Time had simply whizzed by. The first one and a half years had been awesome to say the least. The last part of it pretty much sucked.

I had received the offer letter from the FMCG I had to join and I still had a few months before I would join the company. That meant I would have nothing to do for that time and it scared me. *Nothingness will consume me*, I thought.

Earlier when we were together, Avantika and I had already decided how we would stay together, once again, if our jobs took us to the same city. But these were the least important of our plans. I was already twenty-five and had started to feel a little older than usual. We had never explicitly talked about it, but we knew it was on our minds. We had talked about it in undertones. We had to plan long term—better sooner than later.

'Why don't you call her?' she said when she saw me making circles in the dirt on the canteen table.

'It's not helping. I called Avantika five times in five days, and it is all the same. I can't get it out of my head, I never will. We can never be together again.'

'Why not?'

'I can't forget what happened. There's nothing more to it. I have tried and I have failed. It doesn't work. I can't get over it,' I said.

'What does she say?'

'. . . that she loves me, that whatever she did was a mistake, and it shouldn't matter if I love her.'

'Isn't she right?'

'No. The bitterness will stay. It will always stay. I will never forget what happened and I will never love her the same. I wouldn't ever be able to trust her again. She lied to me. It's better for her that we don't get together.'

'For her? All you are thinking about is yourself. You and your male ego is all that matters to you.'

'I don't know what it is but I just can't be with her. Not right now.'

'Don't make it too late,' Malini said.

'I don't care.'

'You do care. Have you seen yourself? You are a shadow of the guy you once were. Where is that smile that used to be on your face? Where is that cute goddamn dimple? You don't jump around and do the stupid things you used to. You have changed.'

'. . .'

'Just stop being such a jerk. Look at her! Don't you feel sorry for her? She is alone and she cries all day. Why are you doing this to her? She loves you, Deb,' she said.

'Why are you taking her side?'

'I am not taking her side.'

'She slept around, not me! Avantika will be fine. She will go to Mumbai with Kabir and they will be fine,' I said.

'You know . . .'

'Malini? Can we stop talking about it?' I grumbled.

'Fine,' she said. She shut up and we didn't speak a word for the next hour. Malini would put up with my irrational mood swings those days without protest.

'I am sorry, Malini,' I said.

'For what?'

'For shouting at you . . . usually, messing up your life. I didn't want you to get involved in this.'

'If you hadn't noticed, I wasn't doing anything constructive before you came along and I ruined your life,' said Malini guiltily.

'You didn't do that.'

'I did. If it were not for me, you would still be with her. Both of you would have been smiling . . . and look at you. I totally ruined your relationship.'

'. . . that you did,' I joked and smiled at her, '. . . though I like you!'

'You don't have to fall in love with me.' She smirked playfully.

'I need a rebound. I deserve one,' I said. 'Don't you think?'

'Stop flirting.' She smiled.

'Why?'

'Because you are making me feel good,' she said.

'And that is when I haven't even kissed you. I'm told that I'm pretty good at it. Like earth-shattering good.'

'The last time you kissed me wasn't the most pleasant of experiences.' She laughed.

And soon we were talking about our first kisses. She recounted her time in Canada. For the first time, she was utterly chirpy and bubbly and I liked the new side of hers. I asked her what had turned her into the bitch she usually behaved like, and she said it was the guys she dated. *Guys destroy everything. Stupid guys.*

43

It was one of those nights that Avantika and I had always looked forward to; I had imagined how it would be a million times, the farewell night, the last night of our college life.

We had seen the senior farewell night and it was epic. Booze, women, music and everybody at their craziest best. The outgoing batch had danced like there was no tomorrow, which, quite literally, there wasn't. There were last-minute proposals and rejections; there were many casual make-outs too; there were fist fights; there was riot control police; there were angry professors who swore they wouldn't have it next year.

We had lived it before it happened and we had waited for this day. I had only imagined how good Avantika would look in the light pink sari we had picked long ago.

Things change.

She was not there that night. I looked everywhere but I could not find her. I spotted every friend of hers huddling together, hugging each other, posing for pictures, checking the pictures to spot closed eyes, and then posing again till they got it right. Even Kabir was there but she was nowhere to be seen. It seemed like it was not meant to be. I missed her. Sitting on the bench, I drank alone. I just wished things to go back to what they were before, even if it was just for that day.

Shashank and Mittal were with their girls and asked me where Avantika was, and I told them I had no idea. I started to ask around and no one had a clue; no one had seen her since the night before. After about half an hour, a classmate of ours said that she had talked to Avantika that morning. She was leaving for her local guardian's place. *Local guardian?* She had no local guardian. The only local guardian she could go to was in Mumbai. She could not have left? Or had she? Panic set in.

How can she leave? She did not even say goodbye! Am I that unimportant? Is she already over me?

I ran to her hostel room, but it was locked. It was not her lock; it was a lock with an MDI emblem embossed on it. She had given up the room and she was not coming back. If only I had known that the night we fought would be the last night there, I would have done something. My fingers trembled. *Where is she?* I called her up but her phone was out of reach. I wondered if she was already on the flight to Mumbai.

Had our time passed us by? The last time I had seen her in that room had passed? We would never be in that room together . . . never again. The urge to talk was eating me inside. I called her again. Her phone was still switched off.

I didn't know what to do. I started typing a message. I had to write 'call me' or 'I miss you', but I ended up with a lot more. I sat on those stairs with tears in my eyes and Avantika on my mind . . .

If I'd only known . . .
That this is the last time we've met,
I would have stopped the break of dawn.
And stopped the sun to set . . .

If I'd only known
That I wouldn't ever see you again,
I would have framed a picture of you within,
To end my suffering, to end my pain.

If I'd only known,
That this is the last time I sit by your side,
I would have told you how much I loved you,
Keeping rest things aside.

If I'd only known,
That we would never hold hands again,
I would have held them strong,
And never let anything go wrong.

If I'd only known,
That you would stand always by my side,
I would have fought the world for you,
Breaking all the walls through.

If I'd only known,
That your love was true,
If I'd only known that you would come back soon,
I would have waited for you to come by.

If I'd only known any of this,
That you were what I was breathing for,
I would have breathed my last for you,
Seen you enough and bid you adieu,
While all I can do now,
Is sit here . . .
. . . and wait.
Love you.

If I'd only known . . .

Sitting in the darkness, alone, I fiddled with the send button for quite some time. All the nights we had spent together in that room flashed in my mind. I read the message again. I wished I had done something about it. It sucked to let her go.

'There you are,' Malini said as she found me. I saved the message in the drafts.

'You were looking for me?' I collected myself.

'All over the place,' she said. 'You're the only person I know here. Come with me now. Don't spoil my farewell night.'

I opened the drafts folder. DELETE. I hit the button. It asked, 'Are you sure you want to delete this?'

No.

'Let's go,' I said. 'Are you sure you want to go back to the party?'

'Where do you want to go?' asked Malini.

'Anywhere but in college.'

I tried not to look at her. We headed towards my car and left the campus. I just looked at her once for her approval and she seemed to be telling me that she was okay with wherever I wanted to go.

'Missing her?'

'You must just hate me?' I asked Malini.

She was probably the best dressed at the farewell that day, since her only competition had decided not to turn up. Her backless blouse showed every bit of her spotless white back and the tiny straps threatened to come loose any moment. The glittering red sari, with a clutch and the diamond jewellery, made her look like some movie star who had lost her way to the set. I had never seen her in Indian clothes and this was a welcome change. She looked nice and I felt guilty that I had not complimented her yet.

'Why would I hate you?'

'Last night in college and I drag you out here.'

We had driven to a creek near our college that had served as our drinking place for quite some time. Not a soul was around since alcohol was free and aplenty in the college campus for a change. Shashank, Mittal and I used to go there quite often before the Haryana police picked us up a few times on our way back and the bribes became unaffordable. It was an unfinished bridge and had been cordoned off years ago after a couple of bikers had drowned in the water below.

I walked Malini to the edge and we sat there, our feet hanging from the edge of the bridge. Silence engulfed us— except for the crickets, bugs, the sound of the wind blowing through the weeds and the water gushing beneath our feet. The moon peeked from behind the clouds and reflected off the water beneath us. The redness of Malini's lips still shone through all the darkness. Her eyes sparkled.

'You don't have to be sorry. I had no one else there in college. So I don't mind.' She picked up a stone and threw it across the creek. 'By the way, it also means that I had just one person to impress today. But you don't seem to care . . .'

'Aw! You look stunning!'

'It means nothing now,' she said.

'I would have drooled had I not been a little caught up,' I said, trying to make it better. I looked at her once again. She looked amazing. Moreover, I had never seen someone bare so much—navel, oodles of cleavage, a flat stomach—and not look vulgar, quite like those *FHM* and *Vogue* magazine covers.

'Thank you,' said Malini, smiling. I kept looking at her smile, those eyes, and it reminded me of Avantika. I wished she were there. I missed her. I really did. Everything had ceased to make sense without her.

'What happened?' she asked me.

'I just wished she was there this night. We had gone through this night like a zillion times before . . . we never thought it would end like this . . .'

Malini pulled my arm and made me sit closer to her on the edge of the creek. 'Never mind,' she said. 'Things will be fine.'

'I hope so,' I said, wistfully.

'Do you have something to drink in your car?' she asked.

'I did pick up something from the party, I guess. Didn't really see what it was.'

'Let's get drunk and make out, what say?' She smiled wickedly. 'After all, I do look smashing today, right?'

She desperately tried to lift my fucked-up mood.

'Err . . . what?'

'Just kidding. Let's just do the first part.' She laughed out aloud.

I left her at the creek and rummaged through all the clothes, books and newspapers that had accumulated on the back seat of the car. Since there was no Avantika, there was no one to ask me to clean up the car. I looked for the bottle I had thrown in. There was champagne and an unfinished bottle of vodka.

'We have this.' I raised both the bottles in the air as I walked towards her.

'Not bad. Let me see.' She read out the brand of the champagne. 'This will put you to sleep for the rest of the night.'

'What do you mean?' I asked.

'I mean we all know how much you can take. It is not a secret any more.'

'Is it? You are no better. No offence, but we have also seen how you behave when you are drunk.' I smirked. 'I still remember Mumbai.'

'I will give you that.'

We both laughed.

She popped open the champagne bottle and took a huge swig at it. 'Not bad.' She handed over the bottle to me.

I gulped a little. 'Nice.'

44

'Our lives are so screwed up,' said Malini.

We had got drunk, and though we sat in the car to drive back to college, we could not. I was seeing things in twins and even triplets and the road looked like a long, winding snake, dangerous. She had never driven a car with gears, so we were stuck there until the time I could drive. We flattened our seats, kicked open the doors and decided to catch a little rest before we would go back.

'I know,' I said and held her hand.

'Why isn't there a sunroof in your car?' she said, looking up.

'I should get one.'

'At least I could have seen the stars,' she said and ran her fingers on my face.

'You can see me instead of the stars,' I said. 'Though I'm more of a black hole than a star.'

'You go and see Avantika.'

'She is never coming back . . . she is history . . .' I said and held her hand tighter.

'She will never be history. Your lives are intertwined.'

'I am history for her . . .'

'That can never be,' she said.

'Why are we talking about her? Let's talk about us.'

'There is nothing to talk about us,' she said, stiffening up a little.

'Why? Had she not been around, I would have definitely asked you out. You're beautiful and smart and hot and you get me. What more can I ask for?'

'Had she . . . Anyway, I think I would have rather gone out with Mittal than you. But you, too, would have had a decent shot, you know,' said Malini, and smiled.

'Would have had? We still can, Malini.'

'I can't fight with memories of Avantika. And you wouldn't be able to . . . memories of him,' she said wistfully. She stared into the distance, and we fell silent. Time passed and she just lay there in my arms and said nothing.

'Thinking of him?' I asked finally.

'Thinking of us,' she said.

I wished I had a sunroof.

45

After college ended, I was one of the few students who had a three-month break before joining the firm I had been placed in. Many of my classmates had already joined their firms, hung nooses around their necks, belts around their waists and prepared for a life of servitude and low job satisfaction. Shashank had moved to Bangalore for his investment bank job. Mittal had joined the Mumbai office of his company and had started complaining. Avantika, too, had joined the company we had once interned at.

'Nice place!' I said. 'Isn't it a little empty?'

'I know. It's a little too big for me. But I will fill it up,' Malini said as she sat on one of the cardboard boxes, taped and stuffed with her books, clothes, showpieces and what not.

'So how was Canada?' I asked her.

Malini had left for Canada the day after the farewell night for fifteen days. But she was back in town and she had called me because she needed someone to help her shift. I had been waiting for her call.

'It was good,' she said. 'I met old friends, relatives . . . it was fun. I missed Canada, man.'

'Did you meet him and break up, like, officially?'

'We were never together, but yes, broken up.'

189

'So any post-break-up depression?' I asked her.

'Not really . . . it is okay. I have moved on,' she said as she ripped open one of the cardboard boxes and looked for something inside it.

'See.' She handed me a bunch of photographs.

'Aha . . . nice! I don't know how long it has been since I last saw photographs like these,' I said while I went over the pictures. 'Nice.' I handed the bundle back to her.

'So, Deb, what's on the Avantika front?' she asked. 'Did you call her yet?'

'We have moved on. She has stopped messaging or calling. Just one odd message a day. She is fine with herself, I guess. Kabir is there too . . . so maybe they are together. I don't know and I don't want to know. Why are we talking about her again? I have moved on too.'

'Okay, we won't . . . So what else?'

'Boring days . . . and yeah . . . I missed you.'

'Where are you putting up?'

'Remember Nitin?' She nodded. 'I'm living with him. He leaves for office early morning and I pretty much have nothing to do. But he keeps the house clean and doesn't really bother me, so it's fine.'

'Any plans for the day?'

'I am very busy, Malini. I have to go back home, log into Facebook, update my Linked In profile twice in three days and play Angry Birds all day long. I don't think I have time at all.'

'Help me unpack?' Her puppy face made it hard for me to refuse, not that I would have anyway.

'Sure.'

For the next three hours we meticulously unpacked each one of the thirty huge cardboard boxes stuffed with everything from clothes, to mantelpieces, from books to bundles of pictures like the ones I just saw. We crushed the boxes and pushed them down the garbage chute.

'Malini?'

'Yes?'

'I think you need some furniture,' I said. 'People generally like to sit and sleep . . . but then, entirely your choice.'

'Very funny,' she said.

The house was beautiful, but it was bare. Apart from the two beds in the two rooms, the cupboards and a sofa in the living room, the house was empty. No study tables, no chairs and nowhere to put all the stuff she had carried to that place.

'Whose house is this anyway?' I asked her as we boarded the auto to Panchkuiya, the furniture market near Connaught Place. She had requested me to come along and I could not say no. The last fifteen days had been super boring and this was a welcome change, even if it was just buying furniture.

'My maasi used to live here before they moved to Canada. They want to keep it as an investment, so I am using it. It's a nice house.'

'Good for you.'

'Good for them, too. An occupied house is always well maintained,' she said coldly.

The auto driver zipped through the streets of Connaught Place and we reached the market, lined with furniture shops for the classes and the masses.

'*Bas, bhaiya!*' She tapped the auto driver's shoulder to make him stop. She paid him and asked him to keep the change.

'So what all are we looking for?'

'Study table first,' she said and led me into a small furniture shop and asked me to pick one. She stood there with her hands on her waist as I looked at every piece and remarked that they all looked the same. We spent the entire day choosing, haggling and buying furniture of all shapes and sizes. I had absolutely

no design sense so I had kept quiet for most part of it as she
picked out pieces with unparalleled decisiveness. Within a
few hours, she had picked out a couple of study tables, a few
chairs, a few stools that I had no idea where she would put,
a few lamps and other pieces of furniture that seemed pretty
useless and strange.

'I have no idea where you would put what,' I said. 'I think
you should stop now.'

'Deb, shut up. They all fit in.'

'Fine with me. It is your house. Feel free to ruin it.'

'Let's go,' she said.

'Where?'

'Sarojini Nagar. We still have to get cushions, mattresses,
bed sheets, curtains and towels. I will make up a list in the
auto. I'm sure I'm missing something out.'

'You mean there could be more?' I sighed. 'It's going to be
a long day.'

'It's better than waiting for Nitin to come back home,
isn't it?'

'It sure is.'

She grabbed my hand and led me to another auto and
we headed towards Sarojini Nagar. Sarojini Nagar, a famed
flea market, teemed with girls of every age, jostling for space,
fighting with shopkeepers for the best deal, cursing them, and
then regretting that they had bargained too much and lost out.
Everything at Sarojini Nagar is cheap and fake but they did
not seem to care. I felt sorry for the guys who accompanied the
girls and had huge bags in their hands, but within ten minutes
I had three of them in mine.

She frantically flitted from one shop to another and picked
up everything that she could lay her hands on. She drove a
hard bargain; I would look away when she would offer only a
tenth of any shopkeeper's first quote.

Occasionally, she stopped to look for clothes for herself, bangles and the like but other than that, she was pretty focused. We missed lunch and made do with a roadside chaat of *fresh* fruits, which was filling, and that is the best I can say about it.

'Please tell me if we are done?' I asked, exhausted.

'Yes. Finally.' She smiled.

'We are going back now?'

'Sure!' she said. She still did not look tired at all. Where the hell did she get her energy from? I must have dozed off in the auto because I remember waking up to a screaming Malini. She was shouting on the phone at a furniture dealer who said that their guy would be a few hours late.

'Chill, Malini,' I croaked.

'Oh . . . you woke up? Sorry for that.'

'It is okay.'

'Thank you, Deb,' she said and pulled my cheeks.

'For?'

'For helping me with the shopping . . . I wouldn't have been able to do this alone.'

I looked outside. The sun had set and it was evening already. 'I did nothing,' I said groggily.

'You did enough,' she said. 'Go back to sleep.' She put my head on her shoulder and ran her hand over my face. As I dozed off, I heard her whisper to herself, 'I missed you.'

~

We reached her flat and the day wasn't over yet. We arranged the furniture, hung the new curtains, placed the carpets, dusted the floor and I think we did a pretty good job. Her place suddenly looked warm and inviting. It reminded me of her old hostel room, only a lot bigger and less crazy.

'Are we done for sure? Or is there still something you don't like? This, by far, is the hardest I have ever worked.'

'Aw! No, it's done! It looks nice, doesn't it?' She smiled. I agreed with her. It looked like a cosy little place, far from the barren empty flat it was that morning, and now it was stuffed with wood and textile, and was a riot of colours.

'You are good.'

'So are you,' she said and pulled my cheeks.

'But isn't this house a little too big for just you?' I asked her. 'You should look for a roommate. Get a hot guy to move in. That should be fun,' I remarked.

'What do you want to say?'

'I mean get a roommate. I mean it will be a nice time pass, plus the extra money you can earn through rent,' I said even though Malini never needed extra money.

'Oh . . .'

'What happened?' I asked.

'I thought something else,' answered Malini. 'Never mind.'

'What?'

'Leave it.'

'Tell me.'

'It is nothing,' she said as she rearranged the cushions again.

'Tell me.'

'I just thought you were referring to yourself,' she mumbled.

'Me? I should move in?'

She just stared.

Three days later, I moved in. Initially, she was excited and made room for me, but later she advised me against it and said it would not be good for Avantika and me and the relationship. I told her there was nothing left to save in the relationship. I disregarded every plea of hers of not to move in and invited myself to live there. Deep inside, I knew her pleas of asking me to stay away were only half-hearted.

46

'Did you call her?' she asked as she entered the flat. She threw her handbag and the keys on the table; her hair was a mess and she was panting.

'Nope,' I said as I switched the channel.

'Deb? Why didn't you?'

'I didn't feel like it,' I said as I turned up the volume to drown her voice out.

'We need to talk,' she said and closed the door of her room behind her. It had been a few weeks since we had been staying together and it was fun, much better than Nitin and I living together anyway.

'So?' Malini said as she came out of her room in a stringy top and hot pants. It didn't bother me that she pranced around the house practically naked; I had seen her in less clothes in the past two months. She grabbed the remote from me and turned the volume down.

'Hey! Don't do that!' I said.

No matter how much I acted normal, I had still not moved on. The days used to be torturous. The evenings and nights were easier because Malini was around and we always found something fun to do. The last thing I wanted from Malini was to bug me with what used to haunt me every single minute of the day—Avantika.

'Deb, why don't you do something about it? I cannot see you like this. Why don't you just talk to her?' she asked.

'I am not as bad and miserable as you are making me out to be. I am a lot better.'

'Yeah, maybe! But you need to do something fast. I cannot date while I have a male roommate. You know how people talk,' she said and chuckled.

'Why do you need to date? I am here! Date me.'

'Naah! You are not boyfriend material,' she said.

'Seriously, is there a problem because I am staying here?' I asked, trying out a puppy-face expression.

She snuggled up to me on the couch and said, 'Yes, a little. I do not want to get used to you. It is already happening and it scares me.'

'What's the harm if it's happening?' I asked. Over the last few months, Malini had become indispensable, which is not the best way to describe someone's importance but I think it describes it best. Often, she reminded me of Avantika because, before Malini, she was the only person who had cared for me that much. I was a mess when I first shifted in with Malini. I did not wash clothes, threw clothes around, did not know a thing to cook, and yet she put up with all that throughout the weeks we had been together. But lately things were changing and I involved myself in household chores, and it was not because she asked me to do so . . . but because I wanted to help Malini out. Thank her for what she did for me. Even after a long day in office, she would insist on doing everything for me. Sometimes, it scared even me. She was a little too committed to see me happy.

Was I falling in love again? No, I was not.

But I was sure that Malini had feelings for me and that is what scared me the most. After all that she had done for me,

I did not want to break her heart. Three weeks after I moved in, we had decided that we would sleep in different rooms. The late-night 'hug-and-talk' sessions often used to end in awkward silences and sometimes, and only sometimes, sex. We had made out thrice in that period; we were drunk twice. All three of those nights were followed by awkward mornings.

We managed to stick to our rule for a week. However, after that we started sleeping on the couch and even talked to each other on the phone from different rooms.

It was hard not to slip . . . you cannot blame me though. I was attracted to her, and anyone would be. It was miraculous enough that I managed to keep my hands off her for the majority of the time. Moreover, I was single and there was nothing wrong in what I did. Who knew, maybe Avantika was doing the same with Kabir? Maybe they were even living together like Kabir had once suggested to Avantika.

'You don't love me,' she said. 'I will always be a rebound. That's why it's scary.'

'Do you love me?' I asked her.

'I care about you,' she said and ran her hands over my shirt. 'I am stopping myself from falling for you. I would have been in love with you. Maybe, I already am. But this can't be . . .'

'Why love me? I am a loser,' I asked.

'I know you are. You're a chauvinistic, lazy pig. Wish I could answer that. But tomorrow you are calling her up,' she said.

'Why are you pushing me towards her? Maybe it's you I want to be with? Maybe this is how it's meant to be.'

'Didn't I tell you? I cannot compete with her. I am not that strong. And I know you will be the happiest with her,' she said. 'And seriously, I can't take your crying, Deb. Not only does it look silly, and . . . stupid, it hurts.'

'What do I tell her? I mean, I don't think Avantika even thinks about me that much.'

'You know that can't be. She loves you more than anything. You were *the one* for her. Girls never get past that.'

'She doesn't call me, she doesn't message me any more. It is only I who calls her now. I am sick of it and I am sure she is with that bastard now.'

'Why do you say that?'

'She doesn't text or call me any more! Why? Either she's over me, or that bastard Kabir doesn't let her call me any more.'

'Deb, I don't blame her,' she said.

'Why? Because you are a girl and you must have some stupid reason to back her, don't you?'

'She gave you enough chances, Deb. She begged for more than two months. She put up with everything you said to her . . . the taunts, the abuses, the angry tone. What else do you want her to take? She just assumed you would never come back,' she said.

'Never come back? Is that why I call her every five days? To never come back?'

'Have you ever tried to talk to her calmly and not bring up Kabir in your conversations? Have you? Have you tried to understand what she has been going through? Deb, do not fool yourself. I know you stay up nights and read her old messages. Cry. Think. Ponder . . . Then why this, Deb? Just because she made out with a guy she doesn't love? Even we have had sex, for heavens' sake, but you love her . . . and you love her like crazy. Nothing is going to change that. It will always stay in your heart and it will keep killing you unless you do something about it.'

'But—'

'But what, Deb? Stop this foolishness now. Go to her. It's Avantika. She is your baby! Look what you have reduced her to! Why did you do this to her, Deb?'

'She is just fine . . .'

'Call her tomorrow and ask her if she's fine!' she said, broke out of my embrace and slammed the door behind her as she entered her room. I sat there reflecting on what she said. There was desperation and love in her voice.

I got up and walked towards her room and was about to knock when I heard her crying inside. I knocked and entered.

'Are you crying?' I asked.

'Silly question,' she said and wiped her tears. I went and sat next to her. She put her hands across me.

'Try this. Don't blame me if it isn't good enough,' I said. I had made pasta for her that evening, but I could not tell her because she picked the Avantika issue so soon. Such a waste of delicious-looking pasta, all creamy and cheesy.

'Not bad. Impressive indeed,' she said as she ate. 'A little more salt would have been perfect, but I still think it's quite nice.'

'I am learning a few things from you!' I smiled.

'Do you have a sadistic agenda of making all the awesome girls around you cry?' she said, still crying. 'You don't deserve us.'

'I never said you are awesome.'

'I wish I was.'

'Aw! You are the awesom*est* ever!' I said and hugged her.

'Deb, I have longed for a guy who would love me like you love her. At times, I wanted to be her. And had I been a complete bitch, I would have stopped you from going back to her.'

'Why don't you stop me?'

'You belong to her.'

'Umm.'

There was an awkward silence.

'Call her tomorrow,' she said.

'Give me a week.'

'A week it is,' she said and hugged me.

'Deb?'

'Yes?'

She held me close; I could feel her breath on my lips. She said, 'I want to say something to you.'

'What?' I asked.

'Don't answer to what I am going to say. I just want to say this because if I don't, I will never be able to forgive myself,' she said and the tears in her eye reappeared.

'I won't,' I said. 'What is it?'

She put a finger on my lips. 'Deb, please don't go . . . I want you to stay,' she whispered in my ears. She closed her eyes and hugged me.

The last few weeks had been good. They could have been a lot worse. She had saved me. I did not leave her that night. I would never be able to pay back Malini for what she had done for me. She was an angel.

~

Malini had been bedridden for the last three days, writhing, moaning and cursing in pain. No matter what I said, she blamed me and the pasta for it.

'Don't get up. I will get that,' I said as she tried to reach for the thermometer.

It had been three days and the fever had started to subside. Just a viral infection, the doctor said. No food poisoning, I told her, but she would not budge. She still blamed the pasta. It was a strange feeling to take care of someone as usually it was the other way round.

'You are very sweet, Deb,' she said.

'Me? Why?'

'I can never imagine a guy doing what you are doing.'

'Ahh . . . c'mon . . . I did not do nothing,' I said and blushed. 'And anyone would have done the same.'

'Yes, you didn't.' She hugged me. 'You did nothing . . .'

I put her to sleep.

47

'Mittal called today,' I said.

It had been more than a week and I had not yet called Avantika. Malini had recovered from the viral and she gifted me a new watch as a token of thanks for taking care of her. Even though she could do something like that to show the commensurate gratitude, I could not have repaid Malini for what she had done for me. No amount of watches or jewellery could repay that debt. She had done a lot for me.

'How is Mittal doing?'

'Good.'

'First time after college?'

'We have talked about five or six times,' I said.

'Best friends, huh?' She winked. 'What did he say?'

'Nothing much. He is coming to Delhi next week and might stay with us.'

'Deb, can you pass on that jug?' she said. 'He will stay with us? That would be nice. How long would he be here?'

'Not very long. A day or two.'

'You don't seem excited,' she said as she served breakfast.

Malini was a great cook. Since she was a health freak, we did not go out and eat junk a lot those days. She was happy whipping up something new for us every weekend. She even tried to take me out jogging, but I couldn't wake up that early.

'Obviously I am excited,' I lied. I was looking forward to it, but I wasn't excited, not really.

'Umm, you know what, Deb?'

'What?'

'Those three days that I was bedridden?'

'What about those?' I asked.

'Those were the best three days I had spent in the longest time.'

I blushed rather visibly. 'Were they?'

'They were so nice. You used to sit by the chair and hold my hand, stay up all night just in case I needed anything. Sweetest thing ever. I loved the way you took care of me, made me go to sleep, made me laugh and tried to make it all better. I should probably pay you and keep you here,' she said and her voice trailed off.

'Hmm,' I couldn't say anything.

'And I would just hate to snatch all this from someone . . . anyone,' she said wistfully.

~

'Are you serious you don't have a crush on Mittal?' I joked.

It had been three hours that morning that she had been working continuously to clean the flat. She had taken a half day from office just to do that. It is strange how quickly time flies. From cleaning up the hostel room, every time a girl was supposed to walk in, to cleaning up a house, time does fly by and we all learn to grow up a little.

'Yes, I do. Remember that date? Mittal and I? Since then,' she said and winked. 'He is awesome!'

'Oh, good for you.'

'I wish that my crush on him would have made you jealous.'

'Oh, it sure did,' I said.

Malini should not have told me that she had strong feelings for me. At least I would have felt a lot less guilty then, and a lot less confused. Malini had done nothing to drive me away unlike Avantika and she had done a lot for me, selflessly.

Malini had an elaborate menu ready for this asshole. It almost looked like we were a married couple expecting a guest. There was a bang on the door accompanied by a huge shout. Unmistakably it was Mittal.

'Hey!' he shouted and hugged me. He had changed. The sedentary office job had made him fat, the abs had gone, and the buttons of his shirt were straining against his girth.

'Are you losing hair?' Malini said and they hugged.

'You look good together,' he said. 'I always thought so.'

'Umm . . . we are not together,' she said.

'But you guys are making out, right?' He laughed.

'This is for you two.' He handed over a carton of beer bottles. 'Nice house by the way. A little too big, but yeah, it's perfect.'

Malini thanked him for it. 'Deb helped me put stuff in it.'

'So what is going on these days?' he asked us. He opened three bottles of beer and handed one to each of us.

'I am slogging my ass off . . . and he is getting fatter by the day,' Malini said.

'So you actually live here?' he asked me.

'Yes . . . I mean, just a temporary thing till I leave for the job.'

'That I know, but this is where you live?' he asked again.

'Yes. Why?' Malini asked.

'No, I mean . . . is the Avantika chapter closed?' he asked.

'Not really. He will patch up in a few days,' Malini said.

'Anyway, you two continue with your male bonding thing. I have to leave for office.'

'Bye,' we echoed.

'Is that what you wear to office?' Mittal asked and pointed to the short skirt that Malini wore that day.

'Yes, why?' she asked.

'Is there a vacancy in your office?' he said. 'Because I don't give a shit about sexual harassment cases.'

'You have not changed.' She smiled. 'Bye, Deb. I will be late,' she said, kissed me on the cheek and left. Mittal saw that and I saw the expression on his face change.

Ideally, 'the college Mittal' would have given me a high five, but this Mittal shot me a sceptical look.

~

Malini called later that evening and told us she would be late because a petulant client wanted the presentation urgently, and she bid Mittal goodbye on the phone. Mittal was not staying over for the night since he had an early morning flight and his hotel was closer to the airport. He told me how his new job 'sucked elephant balls' and how murderous he felt while in office, and said he missed his college days like hell. He had just bought a new car and a new place but he said nothing would beat the bike rides and the tiny hostel room; I concurred. We drank and discussed the embarrassing and the hilarious bits of our college lives, ran through a montage of incidents in those two years in our heads, and at the end of it, we were drunk.

'You have a slight thing going with Malini, isn't that true?' he said.

'Nope. She has feelings for me, but then she says I need to go back to Avantika. She thinks Avantika is my soulmate or something.'

'What do you think?'

'Malini . . . I mean, she is an awesome person. But I would always be unfair to her and she knows that. I would never forget Avantika, and even Malini has made me realize this repeatedly. But, who knows, I might just get over Avantika some day. Then, Malini and I—'

'I think you should shift out as soon as possible,' he said solemnly.

'Are you all right? I thought you would ask me to go out and sleep with her every night,' I joked.

'If a girl sleeps with any guy for more than four times, she will fall in love with him,' he said and his voice cracked. 'It's the thumb rule and no one is immune. Not even girls who sleep for money.'

'Mittal? What are you saying?'

'Yeah . . .' He looked away, blinking away tears.

'Is everything fine?'

'Nothing is fine, man,' he said as he got up and took a huge swig at his bottle.

'Tell me,' I said, fearing the worst, fearing that he would tell me a sob story and I would have to share his depression and loneliness as well.

'She got married last week, man.'

'She?'

'Nidhi.'

'Nidhi? Who?'

'You don't know her,' he said.

'I know that I don't know her,' I said. 'Wait! Is this the girl you used to talk to in MDI? She was, wasn't she? What happened?'

'I broke up with her when I came to MDI,' he said, almost crying. I wished Shashank were there; he always knew Mittal was hiding something.

'So?' I said.

'I broke up for no reason. She was getting too close to me. Things were getting serious and I chickened out. I went away.

I did not have the courage to take the final step. I was so young and I thought I shouldn't get stuck in all this,' he said and held his head. He almost cried now.

'So this was the girl you talked to? I do not understand. What happened?'

'I loved her but her parents started looking for a guy for her. They asked her if she had a boyfriend; I asked her to say no. She wanted to get married to me, but I did not know whether I could be with her forever. I didn't know that losing her would affect me so much.'

'But didn't you have other girlfriends?'

'I did. I was trying to run from the fact that I loved her. I wished I hadn't.'

'Why didn't you do anything about it?'

'I tried. After she was engaged, I realized what a fool I had been. I told my parents and they thought I was crazy. But they slowly understood that I was serious about her. It was already too late. She said she couldn't leave the guy she was engaged to. She gave me a million chances and I had let all of them go to waste. Not a day passed in college when she didn't ask me if we could be back together. She waited for two long years. I was a fool.'

'What did she say later?'

'What would she say? She made her parents wait for two years. Now, that the ball had started rolling for her wedding, what could she have done? I asked her to come, run away with me, but she said it would be unfair to her parents, and I do not blame her. I was at fault. I was so fucking wrong, man . . . I should have listened to Shashank.'

'Shashank knew?'

'Yes.'

'Why didn't you tell me?'

'You were not in a state to be told anything like this. You

had your own problems, and moreover, you're usually of no help,' he said.

'Who else knows?'

'Avantika,' he said.

'Avantika? What? When did you tell her?'

'I have met her a couple of times. She lives near my office in Mumbai. In Bandra.'

'Anyway, we'll talk about that later. So what happened?'

'What? Nothing, man. I am just ruined. What else?' he said and smiled.

'Are you fine?'

'I am fine. I will just go, screw a few girls, end up alone and die.' He smiled again. 'I hate to say this, but I miss her. Maybe, I will get over her some day, but right now, it kills me.' He continued, 'You know that we are all assholes, right? Except Shashank, of course. We will look everywhere else, and we don't look where we should really look. I mean, she was right there all the time. I mean, are we so fucking selfish? I slept with countless women and she never raised an eyebrow. She never said anything to me. All she wanted was that I should go back to her.'

'It will be okay,' I said. I did not know what to say.

'Deb, I am losing my sleep. To think of her with another guy is killing me. I should have been that guy. I gave it all away. I didn't deserve her. Maybe, it is for her own good. I am sure her husband will love her,' he said and shut up.

Tears streaked down his face and he looked away. Love brings great men to their knees; Mittal was no different. We did not say a word. I am sure we were both thinking about the loves of our lives—Nidhi and Avantika.

I did not want to end up like Mittal. I had seen Avantika with another guy and it felt like death. Suddenly, I wanted to be with her. I wanted to have her in my life and never let her go. Mittal was stronger than me; if he was going through so much pain, I could only imagine how I would react.

What if Avantika finds another guy and I become just another ex-boyfriend in her life? It was a scary thought. I needed Avantika.

~

Mittal left that day with a smile on his face as he always did. But this time I could see what was behind that smile. Regret. Regret that he would find hard to shake off. He told me about Shashank, too; he told me Shashank was trying to convince his parents to let him get married to Farah. Farah's family, on the other hand, was already reconciled to the idea. Shashank would come through, Mittal had said, and he was rarely wrong. Shashank had called me a few times over the last few months but I had ignored his calls. After the break-up, I had lost interest in anything around me.

'What did he say?' Malini asked as she served dinner.

'Nothing much,' I said as I dug into the parantha, which smelled heavenly yet was surprisingly healthy.

'It is okay, if you don't want to talk about it, but I know what is bothering you.' She walked away from the dining table and sat on the sofa.

'What?'

'It's Avantika, isn't it? . . . What if she finds another guy,' she said as a matter of fact.

'It isn't that,' I said.

'Yes. Sure it isn't,' she said sarcastically. I wondered if she was pissed because I was with her, but not really with her. Why would a girl like her fall for me? It was just stupid and made no sense at all. I tried to steer the topic away from Avantika and talk about something else though it really didn't work. I just shut up and ate the delicious paranthas which weren't as appetizing as before. Soon after, Malini said she was sleepy and went to her room.

Needless to say, neither she nor I could sleep. I knocked at her door.

'May I?'

'Yes,' she said. She was reading a book—a thick one, I think it was *The Lord of The Rings* or something.

'I thought you were sleepy.'

'I was,' she said and closed the book.

'Malini?'

'Yes?' she said.

'If Avantika wasn't there . . . we would have been—' I said and stopped midway.

'Deb? You think I am sad because of her?'

'Are you not?'

'No, it's not her. It's just that . . . you will leave in a few days. You will join your job and I will be all alone,' she said wistfully.

'. . .'

'It will be tough for me, you know.'

'It will be tough for me too,' I said.

She continued, 'I have gotten so used to seeing you around. Just thinking that this place would have just me in it makes me sick in the stomach. You know, coming back from office and not seeing you, not seeing the mess around you, not bugging you to go take a bath, forcing food down your throat. I will miss all this.'

'Get a roommate,' I said when I should have hugged her. I wanted to hug her.

'It will not be the same. They don't make cute guys any more.'

'I am cute?'

'The best I have seen,' she said, put her arms around me and pecked me on the cheek. 'I am so spoilt now.'

'You? What on earth have I even done to spoil you? I am the spoilt one here. You need to get your eyes and your mind tested. There's certainly something wrong going on there.'

'You have done nothing. But I guess people just get too used to the idea of you. And the idea of you is brilliant, Deb . . .'

'You are being too—'

'Shut up.'

'If you say so.'

She clung on to me. 'I will miss you,' she said.

'I will miss you too. And I will come and visit often.'

'That you know will never happen,' she said. 'And it should not.'

'It will. I can't live without you.'

'Thank you. You are being so—'

'Shut up.'

I hugged her until she dozed off. I left her seeing her sleep like a baby. It was one of those days when you ask yourself, 'What have I done to deserve this?'

I rarely thanked God for anything those days. But I did that day, for giving me Malini. While she slept peacefully, my mind became a battleground of conflicts. Malini and I. Was there a possibility? She was the sunshine that shone on me when I found myself deep in despair. I liked being around her.

What would it be like not to have her around? I shuddered to think. I tried not to.

48

'You have to pack eventually!' she said.

Over the past week she had been saying this over and again, and I had been delaying it for as long as possible. My going away would have seemed real had I started packing. I wanted it to be an illusion and not accept it for as long as possible. I did not want that to happen soon. I loved this life. This life was good. Being alone would be crazy and depressing and I would feel like clawing my eyes out. I had got used to living with Malini, and hence I avoided packing up my life—it meant I would have to leave soon. Living in denial was a better option. The fact that I would be entering an empty flat without Malini sucked. A new city where I would have to build a life of my own from scratch was not exciting. It was saddening and depressing.

Malini and I had been going shopping every day for essentials, bed sheets, and blankets, everything that she thought I would not be interested in buying on my own and would start living without. But more often than not, we ended up shopping for each other. In the last week itself I gifted her perfumes, numerous pairs of footwear and some other small things that I don't remember. Seven days. Just seven days and I would be miles away from her. The time I had spent with her would be history. I felt sad.

'I will. There is still time! Seven days. It will hardly take one day to pack everything. Moreover, we are not wasting your sick leave in packing.'

Malini had taken the week off since it was the last one with me. I loved her for doing that. I wanted her to do so. I told her that this would make it harder for both of us, but she did not listen. She wanted time with me and so did I. We wanted to make the most of the time we had.

'Come here,' I said.

She came to the couch and held me close. We had spent hours in the past few days like that.

'Deb?' she said. 'Now that I won't be there to distract you, mend it with her.'

'She doesn't care. No calls, no messages even now.'

'But *you* do! You are miserable without her and you will be even more miserable when I won't be around.'

'I will come to visit you. You will make it all better, won't you? I need you.'

'Every day?'

'As if I could be with her every day!'

'It is not the same. She can be around you even when she is not. I can't.'

'You are underestimating what you mean to me.'

'No, I am not,' she said and clung to me harder. I thought she would cry out but she did not. I was sure she cried in her heart. Because I did.

'Why do you keep pushing me towards her? Maybe I don't want to go.'

'If it was to happen with you and me, I would have sold my soul for that to happen.' She smiled and kissed me. Maybe this was what was meant to be. I didn't have to leave her.

49

'I know you love this place,' Malini said. She had booked us a place at the most ridiculously expensive resort some fifty kilometres from Delhi where the rich kids of Delhi would drive off to throw lavish parties other rich kids attended. It was a huge fortress lit so brilliantly I was sure it was visible from far-off alien pods. There were pools the size of football fields, huge banquet halls with dinosaur-sized chandeliers, handsome staff which could be passed as models, buffets that served everything that you might have ever eaten and more; even at sixty grand a night, this place was worth it.

'I don't love this place. I have never been here. I just have heard about it . . . and this is so awesome.'

'I knew you would like it,' she said. It was Malini's farewell gift to me.

'But you shouldn't have spent so much. Had you gone totally nuts? It's so expensive. What did you do? Sell a kidney?'

'How did you know?'

'I checked the price listings,' I mumbled.

'Don't worry about it,' she said and clung to my arm as we walked past a pool, and picked up a wine glass each on our way.

'Are we going to have sex today?' I asked.

'You want to?'

213

'It would be a shame to waste a room which costs that much.'

'Oh, the room? That's why you want to do it? I thought it was something to do with me.' She punched me.

'Obviously, it has to do with you! Or I would have a random girl for it!' I smiled and added, 'Who wouldn't want to sleep with you?'

'Oh yeah?'

'Sure. Let's do it.'

'We will see,' she said.

I had asked the question in good humour but the fact that she had not totally shot it down had me in tingles. We were not even drunk. Somehow, that night I wanted to make out with Malini. I blamed it on the overwhelming emotion that flowed in the air that day. It was our last day together.

'Isn't the food just awesome?' I told her as we found ourselves a huge comfortable couch near the pool.

'Yes it is.'

'Why are you starving yourself then?' I asked.

'I just don't feel like it,' she said.

'Hmm . . .' I kept the plate aside and held her hand.

'Last night together, Deb,' she murmured.

'Why? We have tomorrow night?'

'You have a flight.'

'It is at 2 a.m.! We have the whole night,' I reasoned.

'It's 2 p.m., stupid. Only God knows what you will do there alone?'

'I will be fine. Moreover, I will call you every day! So you can guide me all the time.'

'If you insist,' she said solemnly.

'Don't be sad, Malini. I told you, I will be around . . . We will call, message. You are always on Google Talk or Facebook and so am I. It will not be so bad. We can fly down to meet each other once a month . . . even twice a month. We can afford it.'

'I don't know. Just take care of yourself over there. I will be so worried about you,' she said.

'C'mon, don't be such a mom!'

'Shut up and don't spend days without bathing.'

'Will you stop that already?'

'Okay, just one last thing. Please, please shave on your first day at office. I will call to check.'

'Okay, *Mom*,' I said. 'I will also floss and brush and wipe the toilet seat clean and not let food rot in the fridge. Fine?'

We laughed a desperate laugh, hoping it would hide the sadness that we would not be together any more.

'I had a nice time with you, Deb. I really did. This was not really a relationship but whatever we had, whatever it was, it was beautiful! I just wish it could have lasted.' She smiled.

'Whatever we have,' I corrected her.

'We will see.'

'Nothing has ended, Malini. I am still around.'

Just then, I heard a male voice shout out behind my back.

'DEB?'

I looked around to see the smug bastard Kabir dressed in a sharp suit, staring at me like I was a caged animal.

'Hey! Malini? You guys? Here!' he cried out loud.

'Bastard,' I murmured and Malini hit me.

'Hi, Kabir,' she said.

'Hi,' I said.

'What you doing here?' he asked.

'We come here often,' Malini said. 'You?' Kabir missed the sarcasm in her voice.

'I have an office trip here, an investors' meeting. A lot of my colleagues are here. So what are you guys up to?'

The minute he said it I wondered if Avantika was around, and I looked behind to quickly glance through his office group. Nope, she wasn't there.

Maybe she was in her room. Maybe she had not come altogether. *What if she is here and has seen me with Malini? But then she already knows that I am living with Malini? And Kabir? Maybe they have put up in one room? Is that where she is? Should I go talk to her? No, I should not. I should wait.*

'Why don't you join us?' Malini asked him, much to my displeasure.

'Sure.'

To make things worse he could not even refuse. As soon as he sat down, much to my chagrin, he started with his small talk, and after telling us boring stories of office politics and his professional exploits, he asked what we were up to those days.

'I am working with HUL and he is leaving for his new job in a few days,' Malini said.

'Oh . . . where are they sending you?' he asked me.

'Bangalore.'

'So you have been living here? In Delhi?'

'Yes,' we echoed.

'We live together,' I said. I know why I said that. I wanted Avantika to know, to feel hurt. If at all it mattered to her. But I still wanted to tell her I was doing fine. Kabir would obviously tell her.

'Where were you posted? Mumbai, I guess?' I asked him.

'Yes, though I often shuttle between Delhi and Mumbai.'

'Oh, cool,' I said. I wanted to kick him into the water with weights tied to his ankles.

'So what else?' I asked him. Obviously, I wanted to get out something about Avantika. I just had to know. I prepared myself for the worst. *We are going out. We will get married in a few days.*

'Nothing much. You tell me. What are you up to?'

'Usual boring corporate life,' Malini butted in. 'Avantika is in the same office, right?'

'Yes, but I have never seen her in Mumbai. She is in a different branch so that's in another office at the other end of the city,' he said. 'Been quite some time now.'

'I thought you would know,' he said and looked at me.

'They don't talk any more,' Malini said.

'Oh, I didn't know that,' he said.

It is because of you, asshole.

'So when was the last time you talked to her?' Malini asked.

'I don't know . . . just before leaving college, I guess?'

'And never after that?' I asked.

'Yes, but why?' Kabir asked, a little puzzled because of the questions we threw at him.

'Nothing, just generally,' she said.

Someone from his office group shouted out his name. 'Need to go,' he said. 'Nice meeting you after such a long time. Catch you later.'

We all got up and hugged, and then he left. And following that there was an awkward silence.

'He hasn't talked to her after college ended,' she said. My head was bursting with possibilities and I did not want to talk about it any more. Anyway, just the sight of that guy made me sick in the stomach. It was anyway hard enough to quit visiting his Facebook profile for signs of Avantika.

'How does it matter?' I said, a little pissed off, a little relieved. 'Can we order these things in the room too?'

'Yes.'

'And a movie too?' It was a stupid question since the screen in our room was thrice the size of the biggest television I had ever seen; without movies to rent, it would just be a waste of a big plasma screen. 'And lots of alcohol?' I winked.

'Are you planning to get naughty?' she smirked.

'Could be!'

'I don't mind.' She winked back.

We picked up our glasses and left the table.

'Oh, wait,' she said.

'What?'

'A little girl time,' she said and pointed towards the washroom.

'Cool. I will order everything necessary.'

'Fine,' she said and walked away.

I flipped open the menu in the room and ordered everything that caught my fancy, in the decreasing order of how much it cost. To go with it, I ordered a lot of alcohol. The order was there even before Malini could relieve herself.

As I waited for Malini to come back, I could not help but think about Kabir and Avantika. Kabir had not talked to her ever since that day. I could not shake this off my head. Who was Avantika talking to? I wondered if she was still waiting for me. But she had even stopped calling me. Kabir didn't even know that Avantika and I had broken up. What was Avantika up to?

These words troubled my head and I drank directly from the wine bottle. *Why? Why?* I kept asking these questions. I kept drinking to drown the questions out. Slowly, things had started to blur a little just like I wanted them to.

~

'Seems like you have ordered everything there was on the menu!' Malini said as she entered the room and saw the room stacked with food and alcohol.

'Couldn't help it!' I smiled. 'That's what poor guys do. I might even pack some of this and take it home.'

'Are you already drunk?' She sounded a little miffed.

'Just a little bit,' I said, though my eyes were rolling over. 'Come! Let's have shots!'

We took three shots in a row—hot, disgusting and really, really good, and I really felt like kissing her then; she looked fabulous. She popped the CD in the player and the movie started, *The Truman Show*, and we snuggled up to each other. We sipped on our beers and I was getting wasted; faces in the movie became smudges and the room was suddenly dark, and sort of underwater.

'You shouldn't have drunk so much.' She laughed out.

'Why?'

'We wouldn't be able to make love now! You will fall asleep halfway . . .'

'You challenge me?'

'I sure do, Deb.'

I grabbed her and threw her over on the couch. 'You still have time to take that back,' I said as I ran my hands over her legs while pinning her down by her hand. She looked at me in defiance. Her eyes mocked me as she smiled wickedly.

'I won't,' she said, her lips curved as if to shoo me away. I leaned forward to kiss her and fell on the floor, head first. Luckily, I was drunk, so it did not hurt a bit. She laughed again.

'Okay, now that is a miss,' I said and she smiled.

'You are such a girl. And I don't make out with girls.'

'I want to make out with a girl. And we need to make out, like, right now,' I shouted out. I was clearly drunk.

'We aren't making out! You are getting your girl back,' she said.

'I am not getting anyone back! You are my girl!' I stood tall and shouted out, obviously shaking in my shoes.

'Is it?'

'Yes, Malini! You are my girlfriend now ... and I make that announcement, right NOW!'

'Are you sure, Deb?'

'Sure, AS I HAVE . . . as I have never been before,' I shouted.

'Is it?'

'Yes! Can we make out now? Can we make out now ... just to seal the deal? Can we make out ...' I grabbed her.

'Nah, we aren't making out! Neither did they,' she said, breaking out of my embrace.

'They?'

'Kabir and Avantika.'

'YES! They didn't need to make out! They didn't have to make out! I agree!' I shouted again. Everything had started to get confusing. Words were not registering in my head.

'And they didn't! THEY DIDN'T MAKE OUT! Do you hear me? They didn't make out. They didn't even kiss.'

'What? They didn't? They did!' I said. Alcohol makes your brain cells dead.

'They didn't make out,' she said sternly.

'Yes. They made out! Avantika told me!'

'I just talked to Kabir. They didn't even kiss,' she said.

For a brief moment, I was back to my senses, and then everything blacked out. I passed out. Darkness. *They didn't make out?*

50

I woke up the next morning with a terrible headache. My head was pounding, my throat was dry and my lips were parched.

'Let's go,' Malini said. 'It's twelve.' She was shaking me from head to toe.

'Huh? Oh . . . right.'

Fuck! Flight!

We left that place and took the resort pick up back to the flat. I slept all the way through. My head still hurt and it only became a little better when she made lime juice for me.

'You still drink like a girl,' she said and smiled. She did not say much that day. It was understandable. I had to leave and we weren't happy. I saw those packed bags all around me and it depressed me; I would always miss those months.

'Hmm.'

I was still a little groggy. Everything was still a blur in my head. I put my head on the table and tried to get some more sleep.

'You know what to do now,' Malini said.

'What?'

I did not know what she was talking about until I gave it another thought. Alcohol makes you forget quite a lot of things, but it was not one of them. It was not something I would forget. But I have to admit, it had slipped out of my mind. *They didn't make out.*

'Malini?' I asked and interrupted her while she was packing. There was nothing more to pack. She just didn't want to look at me that day. She had tears in her eyes.

'Yes?' she asked.

'You were kidding last night, right?'

'Kidding? About what?'

'Kabir and Avantika? They made out, right?'

'No, why would I? I wasn't lying,' she said, her voice was serious and cold. She was not messing around.

'Maybe Kabir lied. He is a bastard, right?'

'Is it? You think he is a bastard?'

'Yes! Why? Don't you?' I asked.

'If he was a bastard, he would have told me that he had made out. He would have said that he was still doing so,' said Malini and got back to packing my bags.

'Then?' I asked.

My mind had stopped processing anything. Nothing made sense. Was Malini lying? Was Kabir lying? Was Avantika lying? Why would anyone of them lie? There was someone who was lying here, right?

'Is it too hard for you to get, Deb?'

'What is there to get? Kabir lied, that's it!' I said.

'Kabir didn't lie. Avantika did. She lied about everything,' she said and looked away.

'Avantika?'

'Yes, your girlfriend lied to you! Don't you get it?'

'But why?'

'She was your girlfriend. Figure it out.'

'Did she want to get rid of me?' I asked. Obviously, she did not. Why would she? I was everything to her. Avantika did everything to get back with me. But why would she do it? Why would she lie?

'No, Einstein,' she said, 'she did not want to get rid of you.'

'Will you stop being so sarcastic?'

'Then, what do you want me to act like? Like your girlfriend?' she snapped.

'Why are you snapping at me like that?' I asked. She did not say anything. I sipped on my lime juice and my head was hurting more than before.

'Deb, I am sorry. I am just a little ticked off. I will be okay. But isn't this great? She did not cheat on you! That is what matters. Whatever her reasons may be, she didn't leave you. She never wanted to. It's you who left her.'

'I did not leave her. She did. She made out! She made me leave her,' I defended myself.

'She didn't! She lied. Don't be so dumb,' she said.

'What?'

'Yes, at least it makes a few things clear. You should go and get her; she probably is still waiting for you to realize how much she loved you. Maybe, she is still waiting for you to tell her how much you love me,' she paused and realized the mistake. 'I mean how much you love her. Go, run back to her, go back to her, this is a sign, don't you think so?'

'I don't think so,' I said. 'Why would she lie?'

'Maybe, she just wanted to test you,' she said.

I did not know what to say. Lie? Who would lie about such a thing? Was she testing me? Who would test anyone like that? But if she was testing me, I had failed. I had left her just because she told me that she made out with someone. She used to text me that the relationship meant everything to her. Then, why did she have to lie and finish it? Why did she want to test it? Why the hell would Avantika do so? What the fuck did I do? I just wished in those moments that I had not met Kabir.

'I can't go back to her,' I said.

'Would you be able to live with the fact that you broke up for something she never did?' she said.

'But she told me she did it.'

'And you broke up. That's what she wanted to check!' she said.

'Why would she do that? She knew I loved her,' I said.

'Loved her? That's why you broke up with her so easily?' she asked.

'Umm . . . But why did she do it?' My eyes had welled up.

'It does not matter what she did . . . what matters is what you do now.'

My world just turned upside down. The last few months, I had been blaming Avantika for wrecking my life. But it was a lie. I sat back and my head clouded with thoughts of Avantika and what I had done. Though I had been utterly selfish all these years, in those moments, I really felt I should not be with Avantika. Why does she always have to be right? Why does she always have to be perfect? Why couldn't Avantika have just gone out with Kabir and slept with him? Why did she have to test me? She had made me feel like an asshole. I left her because Kabir had kissed her. Was it all that mattered to me? She made me realize that my love for her wasn't strong. But, why did she have to stop calling me once she went to Mumbai? Maybe, she had given up. She had lost all hope that I would go back to her.

And Malini? Suddenly, my relationship with Malini was based on a lie that Avantika told me. I would rather be alone than be unfair to her. If I were to leave Malini and go back to Avantika, what would it do to Malini? It would be hard for her. She would have nobody. Why did I have to screw up everything? Why did I have to hurt everyone who ever loved me?

'I am doing nothing. I do not deserve her. I have done enough to screw her life up and I am not doing the same again. I mean, I cheated and I left her when she said she did, when she actually didn't. How will I explain this? I lived with you all these months. I have hurt her enough. She doesn't need to be with me. She is better off alone. I am better off alone. At least I will not end up hurting someone.'

'Don't be stupid. You should be with her,' she said and her voice cracked up.

'And you?' I walked up to her.

'I will be fine. I always have been, Deb.'

'I don't want to leave you,' I said and I hugged her.

'You have to. You probably don't want to right now, but you will not regret it. She is your life,' she said. She had tears in her eyes.

'I don't want this to go waste. I don't want us to go waste. I want to stay.'

'I want you to stay too, but it can't be. You cannot change it! And don't worry, I will find someone. Someone better than you!'

'You will?'

'I will never look for one . . .' She clung to me and burst out in tears. We stood there like that for quite some time before the bell rang. It was the taxi. I felt sorry for her. I should have been happy about Avantika and Kabir, but I was sadder for Malini.

'Won't you see me off at the airport?'

'I can't see you go.' She let go of me.

'Won't you wave at me?'

'I will wave at every plane that goes over this afternoon. Wave back,' she said with tears in her eyes.

'I will miss you,' I said.

'I will miss you too,' she said.

We kissed for a few brief moments. We were not drunk this time. It felt good. I opened the door and the driver loaded the luggage on to the lift.

'I have to go now.'

'Yes. Be safe. Careful with your things. And take care. Do eat on time,' she said.

'I will.'

'Bye,' she said.

'Bye. Take care of yourself.'

'. . .'

As I turned around to leave her house, I heard her whisper to herself, 'Love you.' I paused for a few moments outside the door. Everything from the first day I had stepped inside that flat to this moment when I was leaving the place flashed in front of me. I wanted to hug her again for one last time. But the taxi honked; I had to leave. I promised myself, that I would come back for more.

~

As the taxi left the complex, I looked at the balcony where Malini and I used to spend our Fridays with a coffee and each other. She was not there. My phone beeped. It was a message from Malini. The message seemed familiar.

Her message read:

> Sorry to have looked into your cell phone. But then we had nothing to hide from each other. And this seemed appropriate.
>
> *If I'd only known . . .*
> *That this is the last time we've met,*
> *I would have stopped the break of dawn.*
> *And stopped the sun to set . . .*
>
> *If I'd only known*
> *That I would not ever see you again,*
> *I would have framed a picture of you within,*
> *To end my suffering, to end my pain.*

If I'd only known,
That this is the last time I sit by your side,
I would have told you how much I loved you,
Keeping rest things aside.

If I'd only known,
That we would never hold hands again,
I would have held them strong,
And never let anything go wrong.

If I'd only known,
That you would stand always by my side,
I would have fought the world for you,
Breaking all the walls through.

If I'd only known,
That your love was true,
If I'd only known that you would come back soon,
I would have waited for you to come by.

If I'd only known any of this,
That you were what I was breathing for,
I would have breathed my last for you,
Seen you enough and bid you adieu,
While all I can do now,
Is sit here . . .
. . . and wait.

Love you.
If I'd only known.
Bye, Deb.
Malini.

My heart pounded, my brain felt heavy, and my eyes welled up. I tried not to think what she would be doing. She would be crying. I wanted to rush back above, hug her, and do something about it. Anything. I wanted to tell her that I didn't deserve her. Or anyone else. Her. Avantika. No one.

Malini. She screwed me, and then saved me and I gave her nothing. The car drove into the airport and the driver loaded my luggage on to the trolley. I looked at my cell phone and I wished Malini would call, but she didn't. She once told me that she would never call or message once I left for Bangalore. She told me that it had to end some day, and this is how she would end it. She would be out of my sight and out of my mind. I had always thought she was kidding. Probably she was not.

I collected my boarding pass and headed for the waiting area. A lot of flights were being cancelled those days due to bad weather, so Malini had asked me to check for mine before leaving. I had not. I sat there thinking about her. And Avantika. She lied and I failed her, just as I had failed Malini. I finished everything.

Avantika would not take me back. Why would she? Had I loved her, I wouldn't have left her. *Maybe I should just stay alone for a while*, I thought to myself, *and not destroy any more lives*. I glanced up to see the flight schedule. Two flights stood out. A flight to Bangalore meant a new life. The flight to Mumbai meant the old one—Avantika.

BANGALORE	MDLR AIRLINES	2.00 P.M.	CANCELLED
MUMBAI	INDIGO	2.15 P.M.	DELAYED

I stood there staring at the flight chart. Bangalore—cancelled. Bangalore—cancelled.

I kept looking at the board. Malini had asked me to call her once I boarded the flight. There was no flight now. My eyes kept shifting from Bangalore . . . to Mumbai . . . Mumbai. Should I tell Malini about the flight and go back to her? Or catch the next flight to Bangalore? Or should I get on the flight to Mumbai?

I flipped open my cell phone and dialled a number; selfish as I always have been. We are allowed one big mistake in our lives, aren't we? I was being selfish again, I was being Deb again, and I was being spineless again. I dialled the number. The phone rang.

'Hey,' the voice said from the other side.

'Hi, Avantika.'

I looked up the flight schedule board. The words, the letters, the numbers . . . everything became clear.

MUMBAI   INDIGO   2.15 P.M.   DELAYED

'Where are you?' Avantika asked.

'. . . minutes away from a flight to Bangalore,' I said. I wanted to get out of the phone and hug her. I wanted to kiss her and make her mine again.

'Oh, new job. Best of luck,' she said. It was such a pleasure to hear her again.

'Thank you, Avantika,' I said.

'So when's your flight?'

'I am thinking of missing my flight,' I said. I had not decided what I would say when I made that call. But as I talked to her, it became clearer.

'What? Why?' she asked.

'. . . I am coming to Mumbai,' I said.

'Mumbai? Why?' she sounded genuinely shocked.

'I met Kabir,' I said. 'I know you lied.'

'. . .'

'I know you love me,' I said, '. . . and I love you.'

'What if you hadn't met Kabir?'

'Sooner or later, I would have run back to you,' I said. She was not convinced by what I had said.

'Sooner? It's been three months, Deb,' she said and her voice started to crack.

'The next flight to Mumbai leaves in an hour. I should get a ticket!' I said.

'But—'

'We will talk when I get there!' I said.

She was still talking when I cut the phone. She didn't want me to come, but I didn't care any more. I looked at the girl at the ticket counter and she smiled and said, 'One ticket to Mumbai? An angry girlfriend, I suppose?'

'Yes, please!'

I took the ticket and walked away from the counter. The ticket-counter girl shouted from behind, 'Go! Get her!'

If It's Not Forever
It's Not Love

Durjoy Datta • Nikita Singh

To the everlasting power of love . . .

When Deb, an author and publisher, survives the bomb
blasts at Chandni Chowk, he knows his life is nothing short
of a miracle. And though he escapes with minor injuries, he
is haunted by the images and voices that he heard on that
unfortunate day.

Even as he recovers, his feet take him to where the blasts
took place. From the burnt remains he discovers a diary. It
seems to belong to a dead man who was deeply in love with
a girl. As he reads the heartbreaking narrative, he knows that
this story must never be left incomplete. Thus begins Deb's
journey with his girlfriend, Avantika, and his best friend, Shrey,
to hand over the diary to the man's beloved.

Deeply engrossing and powerfully told, *If It's Not Forever . . .*
tells an unforgettable tale of love and life.

You Were My Crush
Till You Said You Love Me!

Durjoy Datta • Orvana Ghai

Would you change yourself for the love of your life?

Benoy zips around in a Bentley, lives alone in a palatial house and is every girl's dream. To everyone in college he is a stud and a heartbreaker. But is he, really? What no one sees is his struggle to come to terms with his mother's untimely death and his very strained relationship with his father.

Then once again his world turns upside down when he sees the gorgeous Shaina. He instantly falls in love but she keeps pushing him away. What is stopping them from having their fairy-tale romance? What is Shaina hiding?

It's time Benoy learned his lesson about love and relationships . . .

Till the Last Breath . . .

Durjoy Datta

When death is that close, will your heart skip a beat?

Two patients are admitted to room no. 509. One is a brilliant nineteen-year-old medical student, suffering from an incurable, fatal disease. She counts every extra breath as a blessing. The other is a twenty-five-year-old drug addict whose organs are slowly giving up. He can't wait to get rid of his body. To him, the sooner the better.

Two reputed doctors, fighting their own demons from the past, are trying everything to keep these two patients alive, even putting their medical licences at risk.

These last days in the hospital change the two patients, their doctors and all the other people around them in ways they had never imagined.

Till the Last Breath . . . is a deeply sensitive story which reminds us what it means to be alive.

Of Course I Love You
Till I Find Someone Better

Durjoy Datta with Maanvi Ahuja

Let love be your guide . . .

All Debashish cares about is getting laid. His relationships are mostly short-lived and his break-ups messy until he falls in love with the beautiful and mysterious Avantika.

When she returns his feelings, he is thrilled. However, his joy is short-lived as Avantika walks out of the relationship. A broken-hearted Debashish plunges into depression and his life takes a dizzying downward spiral. He finds himself without a job, friends, or a lover. Loneliness strikes him hard.

That is when his friend Amit comes to his rescue and they start putting the pieces of his life back together. Things begin to look up, but Debashish is still pining for Avantika.

Will she come back and make his life whole again, or will he continue to pay for his mistakes?